A NEW NOVEL

THE GOLD ILLU$ION

"Summer Rains"

By:

Allen James Gourley

Rain Falling On Bells

THE GOLD ILLU$ION: *"Summer Rains"* (January 31, 2015)

AUTHOR'S MANUSCRIPT FIRST EDITION (1.1)

Bottom back cover contribution: **Domino Kimiko Gourley**
Strategic overview: **Tiffany Lyne Gourley**

All Biblical verses used: King James Version [KJV] of the Bible.

THE GOLD ILLU$ION: *"Summer Rains"* / Allen James Gourley

Heartfelt thanks to:
Pre-Edit: Talon Gourley, Faith Gourley, Alexander Gourley
2nd Edit: Mr. Leonard Cherico
Professional Edit: Toni @ *FirstEditing*

ISBN-10:1523366575
ISBN-13:978-1523366576

Dedication

GOD ALMIGHTY has blessed me with the most wonderful family - my parents, brothers, and sisters - on both sides of the water. Without them all would surely have been lost. My beautiful wife has loved me without regard to my quirkiness and foibles and, through many cold winters and delayed springs, has graced me with her unwavering love and the gift of three energetic and brilliant children who keep both of us alive and dancing into the future.

And dance we shall, into our blessed and joyful future, as *Children Of Light*.

" It is not who loves you ...

but why they love you! "

Mr. Rains

Table of Contents

Chapter One

He allowed the gauges to fall away from his hand as he absorbed the dire warning they proclaimed so clearly...

He had twenty-two minutes to live.

Deflating his buoyancy compensator, he sat upon a small reef outcropping and allowed his fins to settle into the coral rubble ocean floor to stabilize his newfound perspective on life.

That is, what was remaining of it...

Imminent death has a clarifying ability to transcend all other things.

Yesterday's lingering problems and tomorrow's worries no longer had any bearing on the now he found himself within.

Now was all that mattered; yesterday was a faded memory and tomorrow had yet to exist.

Huge billows of massive waves pushed down into the crystalline waters from above, like rogue liquid clouds they exploded against the outer pinnacles of rock shards that dared to breach the ocean's surface and do epic battle with the winter swells that had marched thousands of miles to explode against them.

Surfacing into that foaming maelstrom would be suicidal at best.

Poor planning and a lack of attention to detail had brought him to this. Any choice, but the right choice, would lead him to instant death. Or, even worse, lingering tortuous death.

Death being the common thread...

He'd become separated from his scuba diving partner, lost his bearings, and no longer knew how to get home. Only one direction was correct, the others would sweep him into currents that could not be managed or controlled.

Being swept out to sea, in this vast ocean wilderness, death occupied a certain portion of his mind that he wished not to go to. So instead, by concentrated effort, he allowed his spirit to soar.

He would not allow the facts to overcome the joy bursting forth in his spirit.

Ultra-clear crystal blue waters surrounded him with liquid perfection. He watched see--through glass minnows barely two inches long in tight swarms and schools of pelagic predators that chased their miniature counterparts relentlessly for both food and sport. The dance of life was on rampant display.

Brilliant bursts of color from the hodge-podge coral forest clung to the surfaces of the small canyons and ridges from every possible angle, even upside down as they appeared to know not the confines of gravity in this effervescent, three-dimensional world.

It was dead calm with absolutely zero current. How strange! Somehow the exploding chaos thrashing above by the incessant winter swells of rolling thunder did not affect the surreal calm enveloping this tranquility of liquid beauty.

Unsurpassed beauty!

Otherworldly gorgeous, it was so awesomely pretty that for a time he allowed the ticking of the clock to be completely pushed aside...

Ticking that grew ever closer to the last breath he would have to enjoy as his air supply relentlessly wound down to a terminal point of finality.

Yet, he would not allow that fact to steal this great truth from him.

This was the most beautiful dive he'd ever experienced in the most astoundingly pristine setting. That reality was worth embracing into the very core of his being.

So he did.

It was a profound choice that overrode all other lesser paths.

His name was Joshua Snow and he now had twenty-one minutes to live.

Today, in the living now, Joshua was searching for the wealth to be found in the spirit of adventure. And, he had certainly found it.

Sometimes you have to be brave to be full of joy. This was certainly one of those moments...

* * * * * * *

Joshua had taken a long route to get to where he was. Throughout his journey of chasing the riches of the world, he was about to stumble, quite by accident, into the adventure of acquiring true wealth.

At twenty-two years of age, unremarkable in either looks or stature, Joshua found himself facing one more epic choice in his world: attend grad school or choose to do something completely out and away from the cloistered world he'd been immersed within for all of the days of his life.

Staying in academia had all of the right elements for him to embrace.

These elements were so hard to overlook: comfortable surroundings, familiar faces like-minded friends, all known quantities and qualifications for remaining within the confines of a reality he'd been groomed for since birth.

"Get a good education" was the mantra all of his mentors; Joshua did not know, nor was he exposed to, any other possible path.

As he'd been taught, via studies in classic and ancient philosophies, knowledge is power. Therefore, an abundance of knowledge would lead to an abundance of power. Obviously it must be a linear equation.

Yet, he kept experiencing moments of extreme doubt that what he was being taught simply was not true.

After all, if an abundance of wealth was to be found in academic knowledge, why on earth did his professors look like the walking dead?

Why did they have distant desires hidden in the depths of their eyes?

Each hid it in their own way, as best as they possibly could.

But yet, in flashes of profound truths, it was there to be seen. Not to be seen but for the glimmer of the faintest of moments, yet there nonetheless.

Once Joshua caught the telltale signs of the lost souls that hid their profound desperation so well, he began to notice it ever more often.

With this sweeping and flagrant knowledge a terrible sadness invaded his world. Eventually this sadness became too much of a weight to bear. This sadness made him aware that all he'd pursued, the riches of perceived knowledge, the knowledge of the world, was a deathtrap unlike all others.

And he realized, that one day, he too would join the wretched ranks of the walking dead.

Yet old habits die wretched hard deaths of their own that he'd become entrenched within.

His university's library was where he would go to study, it was the habit of comfort that encased the very tempest he found himself within: If knowledge was power why did he feel so helpless? Empty and wanting? Storm tossed?

Why was he alone in a sea of fellow travelers?

As Joshua's epiphany grew, that knowledge might not be as powerful as proclaimed he also started to notice a trend within the eyes of not just the professors, but within the eyes of those he walked so willingly amongst, his fellow students.

They too had eyes with scars buried deep within their souls, and tears of jaded forlorn indifference buried as shadows on a vacant horizon.

Despair hidden, yet hoping to be found by someone, anyone that would only take the time to care.

Turning, half-running to vacate the library he'd lost trust in, he ran headlong into her.

Her name, he would eventually come to know, was Summer Rains. She was re-stocking the shelves for minimum wage and chance encounters.

* * * * * * *

While taking courses Joshua needed to attend during the fall semester, he fell into the fine young Miss Summer Rains' eyes and never once considered looking back.

She stunned him with her beauty – then she slowly, methodically would slay him with her love.

5

For Joshua, eventually being slain by the only girl he'd ever love was his first real encounter with the breath of the divine and his first whispers through the echoes of time that heaven actually existed.

* * * * * * *

Sitting at the bottom of the ocean, suspended in a turquoise world of indescribable beauty, can be beyond breathtaking; it is downright mesmerizing.

Joshua looked at his depth gauge fluctuating between 65-97 feet; the waves cascading over the pinnacles high above must be horrendous.

He had always been a quick study in math. Glancing at the gauges, he realized he had twenty minutes of air remaining.

Chapter Two

Loving parents and a *small* family fortune had allowed him to be here. Since his Ivy League University known as Harvard, had such fabled past, Boston had certainly become his favorite town!

He was from the rural forest of Western Pennsylvania. When Joshua described Boston to his childhood friends he referred to it as a fabled city with depth of character and compact cobblestone streets where history walked.

Depth of character undoubtedly, yet soulless frustrations of purloined loneliness embraced the people that lingered too long or failed to grasp the inferiority of the lights of the city that tried its best to never allow them to leave.

The wise fled to other parts of the globe as their mission expired. The unwise remained trapped in the frozen slush of the winter rain.

Joshua would most likely have been one of the forever-lonely souls if it hadn't been for her, Miss Summer Rains. She rescued him with a single question, a quote really from the most divine text he'd come across in his entire life: Inspirational letters of truths, deeply embedded in the annals of time, but mostly forgotten by modern society and the hustle of mankind upon a failing world hurtling through the darkness of space.

After the crash of his lunging into her overstocked book cart, which scattered books down three aisles, he looked to see who he was helping with the mess he had made.

That is when he saw her and fell into her eyes.

After the strangest pause he'd ever been captured by, she had the audacity to stop, lift him up before her, look into the furthest reaches of his overwhelmed spirit, and ask a singular question. *"**Who is this that darkenth counsel by words without knowledge?"***

She posed the question while pirouetting with her hands in a sweeping motion at the vast storehouse of books, voluminous beyond comprehension. Then she looked directly at him and turned her eyes upon the very books held within his arms.

Her question, posed as she'd twirled with an elegance rarely seen, pierced his heart with the first glimmer of wisdom he had been exposed to in over six semesters.

She knew it, of course, and then she dismissed him and walked away. Being the diligent employee, and wishing to righteously earn her minimal wage, she went back to stocking shelves with books of the world.

Joshua had been harpooned with one glance wrapped in a question that he could not answer.

It perplexed him to no end.

* * * * * * *

Like a squadron of fighter jets on a hunter-kill mission, a tight V formation of amber jacks swooped out of the thundering chaos high above Joshua and dropped at an oblique angle into a school of glass minnows. That school of thousands expanded, absorbed the incoming missiles of silver bullets, then reformed behind them. How many were missing after the assault was impossible to tell. Yet the beauty of the dance was spellbinding.

Joshua could not believe the intricate ballet being performed all around him, not just from above, but also on the very reef bench he so easily sat upon. He couldn't help but notice the tiny world, every bit as majestic as the aerial theatrics above, that performed at the tips of his flippers.

A whole family of barber pole shrimp survived around the miniature cave they had commandeered as their castle fortress. The obvious patriarch of the clan fiercely guarded that tiny opening into the coral, being nearly two inches in diameter. It was his domain, and none shall enter. His little ones survived under and around, scavenging as they might while being protected by the father who was mighty in his presence and tiny in his stature.

* * * * * * *

It was over two weeks until he found her again. She was high atop a rolling ladder putting books back that some student had the audacity to find. Why anyone would wish to remove a book from a shelf fourteen feet off of the ground eluded him.

Why she would risk her life putting that book back in the proper place eluded him even more.

Why he searched her out did not elude him at all.

"I found your quote from our last encounter," Joshua called up to her.

"Then bring it up here to me and help me reach this shelf. The boy who had the ability to retrieve this bit of man's knowledge must have been considerably taller than I am."

She laughed as she looked down upon him with those eyes of mystery.

He stood beside her within seconds, forgetting the fact he was afraid of heights.

She made him forget everything that was of no substance. With her he only knew desire.

"So you found my friend, Job?" she asked with dancing eyes that simultaneously looked through him, beyond him, and within him.

"**Job 38:2**, it appears that you quoted the **King James Version of the Bible**, so old-school of you," Joshua answered.

On that rolling ladder platform, with Joshua by her side, with carefree abandon, she pirouetted once again and stated in a voice of a saintly angel. "So much knowledge, so little wisdom." Then with powder blue eyes of wonder, robin egg blue eyes – so rare – she looked at her valiant suitor and asked, as only she could, "Do you wish to know a secret?"

It was mischievously and profoundly posed.

"Yes," was all he could say.

Summer once again motioned at the cavernous works of man in the library that was over 400 years old. The library held millennia of man's knowledge bound and ready to be absorbed by anyone who could read. The fine young Miss Summer Rains looked directly into Joshua's face and said, "All of these books are virtually infinite works of man, facts and theories and variants of both – but yet – truth does not reside within their leather bound pages."

After a long pause...

"So where is truth?" asked Joshua after the long pause to regroup and at least appear to be the brilliant student he had always been told he was.

"Man deals in facts – but GOD deals in truths." She answers with a response that had no rebuttal. "Did you not glean that from your research of our last encounter?" Then she did what he would never forget: she reached up, held his face gently in her hands, consumed him with her eyes, and asked,

"Are you here in search of man's knowledge, or is your search for His wisdom?"

"His wisdom," he stammered.

"Then follow me – I have a secret."

So Joshua found himself following his *library angel* down the halls of knowledge in search of the isle of wisdom he obviously never knew existed.

Through the maze of one of the largest and most in-depth libraries on the face of the earth, within the miles of corridors, was a sacred room. As they opened the air-locked climate controlled door, it was impossible not to notice the display immediately before them. It was a Guttenberg Bible under glass with special lighting and an aura of ancient importance.

She walked past it with reverence, but not without an inspired observation of fact: "God's wisdom condensed. Inspiration for all of mankind is contained in a single love letter so all may know Him."

She looked over her shoulder with a seriousness to make sure she had gotten her point across. Then she continued on, taking him around the bend and further down the corridor to a newly laid out section of this hidden vault of a room.

"Here they are. Just in from a treasure trove found at the furthest reaches of the earth." She smiled with a childlike fascination. "Behold! Ancient texts filled with newly re-discovered wisdom for a world in desperate need of what is to be found within these sacred scrolls, bound in crystal tubes, for such a time as this."

"Wow, how did you know they were here?" asked Joshua, stunned by the wall of hardened glass tubes covering the towering wall before them.

"I seek truth, and it appears in the strangest of places," she answered, in awe herself at the well-lit wall before them. "The real secret isn't that they are here, it is the wealth to be found within them that matters."

For a while time stood still as they contemplated the treasure within their reach.

Like a little boy fascinated, Joshua asked, "Now what?"

"Find the *Scroll Of Courage* and have the courage to read it. Then pick your favorite twelve passages within its matrix, hand write them onto a sheet of paper, and read them aloud into the world. Do it three times a day for three days. Do it someplace majestic and care not who hears or listens." She stated spoke with no room for barter or reason.

Joshua nodded, mesmerized by the location and the brilliance of her response.

When he turned, she was gone, leaving him alone in his quest for wisdom instead of mere knowledge.

* * * * * * *

He snapped back to the present moment. His memories of his first real time spent with Summer Rains flooded into his mind with one of the strangest mornings he'd ever encountered. It was profoundly strange, much like the liquid world he was immersed within.

Intently focusing his attention on his breathing, he took a look at his combination depth and pressure gauge array. He had – more or less – eighteen minutes to live. The only dilemma would be if he allowed the facts to steal away from the truth of the matter.. After all, he'd arrived here, and that fact allowed for the truth that surely there was a way back out of this ocean grotto maze.

Chapter Three

He found a crotchety old librarian, the epitome of a cranky bitter woman who had lost her way to the life stolen from her, and asked her to be allowed to retrieve the *Scroll Of Courage* from the glass tube in which it was encapsulated.

She begrudgingly agreed to allow him to handle "her" treasure. But only if he wore white silk gloves and carefully handled the ancient text with reverent hands and diligent methods.

She hovered over him like an owl reluctantly sharing its winter sustenance.

Joshua unrolled the scroll written on sheepskin in the blackest ink with the most elegant calligraphy he'd ever seen. It was written in a language he could not identify, so he asked his hovering guardian if she could understand the text.

Her answer , more of a barking reply, was short, "It's Paleo-Hebrew. Don't you kids know anything anymore? When I was here, we actually deserved to be here."

He dared not ask her any more questions since she scared him half-to-death. So he did what all 21st century students would do, he whipped out his iPhone and took pictures of the ancient text and left her presence as quickly as possible. He would complete his assignment away from the presence of the vulture hovering over him.

He felt like he'd barely escaped with his soul intact as he fled the corridors of knowledge with his captured bits of truth. Ancient information had been digitized and was ready to be retrieved by the most modern of methods.

That irony did not elude him.

* * * * * * *

Fortunately, the app for translating Paleo-Hebrew into modern English had already been uploaded for any and all to use as needed. Joshua found it posted by Rabbi Yurri Goldberg from the Hebrew University in Israel. Using the photos he'd taken of the *Scroll Of Courage* and the app to digitize it for the needed conversion, he was able to realize the first step in his quest to complete the task given to him by the fine young Miss Summer Rains.

Once done, the translation took but a twinkle of an eye and the gleaned knowledge lay before him, condensed wisdom of the ages in a format and language he could grasp hold of and linger over.

He needed twelve verses, so he pondered and chose the twelve that "spoke" to him.

At The Common, under the morning haze and without fear of strangers within earshot, Joshua read aloud the words to any who would hear.

He did it without care or worry – and especially without fear. For a scroll named Courage could only be read with a sound voice devoid of trepidation.

Then he returned and did it again at high noon to a larger crowd. Then, as per instructions, he returned and performed the required task to the evening crowd, which gathered around him and listened to the words he thrust as truth into the gathering darkness.

Three days later he was back in the halls of the vast library looking for his mentor, his guide, his awesome powder blue eyed fellow traveler.

Little did he know that his courage was just beginning.

* * * * * * *

She looked down at him from the perch of the rolling ladder with a seriously kind smile, and asked, "Did you perform the task assigned?"

Joshua answered, "Yes! Yes I did."

"And, young Mr. Joshua, what exactly did you learn?" Summer carried the conversation to the next level.

"That true courage is wrapped in wisdom and performed with love...." Joshua had a faraway look in his eyes, as he finished his thought, "And performed with love, no matter the costs."

Summer gave a gentle sigh; her eyes danced with the joy at his correct response, so she took it one step further with her divine appointment before her. "Then it is time for you to put your newfound true knowledge to the test. You should perform one act of courage. Something you would have never dared to do just a few short days ago."

Without hesitation, Joshua spoke from the deepest part of himself, the very core of his being. "If that is the task at hand, my bravery shall be put to the test immediately. Young Miss Summer Rains, would you please do me the honor of allowing me to escort you to a dinner and a movie?"

She was stunned by his response, and saw by the fidgeting of his feet and the trepidation of his voice that bravery and courage were both on full display by this simple act wrapped within his question.

So answered, "Yes. I will be happy to join you for such an evening of dining and entertainment."

His startled look contained more information than the vast amount of books that surrounded them.

"Yet, by then it will be prudent for you to complete your next assignment: to find the *Scroll Of Light*. Extract twelve excerpts that speak to you, and then read them three times a day for three days, just as before. But this time do it somewhere on campus where your fellow students congregate."

Summer turned with a smile and walked down an aisle to continue her endless mission of replacing books of limited information.

Joshua didn't remember leaving the library for his next class, as his mind and spirit soared to heaven. As all he could hear was her "yes" echoing in his mind.

* * * * * * *

The gnarly withered vulture of a librarian still gave him the creeps in every possible way, yet Joshua "braved up" while he endured her stares and her grizzled glare as he donned the silk gloves and photographed the *Scroll Of Light* from the bounty of the crystal tubes with the ancient texts towering above.

Carefully he re-rolled the scroll and handed it back to the wrinkled lady that gruffly took it out of his hands and watched him leave her presence.

Joshua willingly left straight away to a happier locale to reconfigure the *Scroll Of Light* into modern English. With his app - *Paleo-Hebrew to English* - the translation took less than a second of time.

* * * * * * *

Using the ancient methods of intentional breathing employed by the Shaolin Masters, a tiny portion of which Joshua had learned in his Aikido martial arts class - a one credit class that he needed to take to fulfill a portion of his Phys Ed requirements - he tried to make time stand still as he breathed at a greatly reduced rate. He allowed his exhales to climb into the chaotic thunder of the relentless crashing overhead. Joshua took careful stock of his surroundings; schools of minnows still made strange shapes, the pursuit of the amber jacks came and went with fierce dynamics. And, best of all, the tiny barber pole shrimp still danced at the entrance of their kingdom with wild abandon.

All this as the sea roared, the ocean pulsed, and beauty immersed his spirit.

Looking down at his gauges, with slow methodical intent, time did appear to have stopped. He still had eighteen minutes to embrace the effervescent stunning liquid world; then he would have to make the final choice of which path to choose. That pathway was far from clear.

Every single trail before him appeared to lead to a most certain terminality. Especially up – and up was where humans tended to live longer than eighteen minutes since compressed gases weren't needed to breathe.

Chapter Four

Joshua stood in the very center of Harvard's Old Yard and announced his presence to all that would hear, three times a day: morning, noon, and night. He read the twelve passages from the *Scroll Of Light* that spoke to him.

Boldly he spoke them aloud to any who cared to listen. By the third day, for the noon reading in particular, he had quite the audience. He even gained a heartfelt standing ovation from the students and faculty gathered. It appeared that courage had its rewards and light had its virtues.

* * * * * *

Six battle-hardened giant trevallies, locally known as ulua, burst onto the scene. Coming from the foaming white rolling thunder above, out of the clouds of foam, they swept across the reef like a pack of rabid beasts; hunger was their one and only motivation. Bits and pieces of yellowtail amber jacks, formerly the hunters – now the hunted - fell towards the protected lagoon's ocean floor.

One tattered tail landed beside Joshua. He kicked it over beside the barber pole shrimp, nudging it just a few inches from the family of ecstatic bottom dwellers and their newfound bounty.

With observational skills on full alert, Joshua deduced that the incredibly fast ulua had to have come from the open waters. In this liquid three-dimensional space, he now knew two out of six ways not to go.

* * * * * *

"So, shall we talk about light?" Summer asked with a smile. "What did you learn? And, if you should be so kind, give me one example that spoke directly to you." Summer's powder blue eyes were filled with fire and mystery.

Joshua got so lost in the depths of her eyes that he asked for her to repeat the question, so she did. But this time as she crossed her arms and tapped her foot.

Summer did not suffer fools easily.

"I loved the line: *Light was the creation and overwhelmed all with its glory.*"

"And...?" Summer probed with an unchanged demeanor.

"My favorite bit of knowledge that I learned, well actually more than knowledge, shall we call it a divine truth: *Light cannot be purchased, bribed, or stolen. It only knows freedom unbounded by man.*"

Joshua's green eyes conveyed his epiphany, as he added, "I had never even considered the implications of those basic simple attributes of light. That light itself is a divine truth from time immortal." Joshua allowed the phrase to linger in the air.

A comfortable silence permeated the library corner where Joshua had found Summer , once again, as she struggled with the ladder that was heavily worn, having wheels that forever refused to roll. All while restocking the shelves with books.

"When shall I come for you on Friday evening? And where?" Joshua asked as he once again reverted to his schoolboy persona, shuffling the floor before him with his foot. Being brave still was most difficult when it came to the brilliant young lady before him with her massively intimidating eyes.

Her eyes lit up even more, as she reveled in his flagrant discomfort, "Five will be fine."

"Where do you live?" Joshua asked with a strange mix of both joy and shock.

"Above the candy store on Newbury. I'll ring you in if you are on time," she laughingly added. She continued the work of replenishing the shelves with books that contained facts – but so little knowledge – and even less wisdom.

Joshua floated upon the air of his newly created cloud of ecstasy. Amazed that a gorgeously stunning girl like the fine young Miss Summer Rains would ever acknowledge his existence, let alone grace him with her presence.

Then it dawned on him that she lived at the most expensive possible address. The candy store she lived above was ultra-expensive. Summer Rains created an epiphany of total surprise, not only was she wealthy, but she lived on *Candy Mountain*!

Chapter Five

Three hugely massive concussions permeated the aquatic reality that he found himself so elegantly trapped within.

Then four...

Then five...

Watching the sand dance across the tips of his fins was surreal. Every time the open ocean waves cascaded across the broken rock formations high above, their concussions made the sand bounce straight up a few inches with their hydrodynamic forces. All the tiny barber pole shrimp dove for cover into their miniature cavern home with the patriarch of the clan guarding the entrance by pressing his eight legs firmly into the bottom and bracing with his antennae against the top for added strength.

As the leader of the pack, nothing was to breach the entrance, not even waves of immense proportions.

Yet, where Joshua found himself, sitting on the ledge of lava rocks and brilliant coral formations, he had zero current. This was strange given the foaming storm of white water above and the sand prancing across his fins set firmly onto the bottom.

Glaring at his gauges and using his very honed skills of quick mathematical deduction, he had exactly seventeen minutes of compressed air remaining.

Give or take a few breaths...

* * * * * * *

Joshua had not seen her since the date, and that was ten days prior. When he had asked her for her phone number – she'd only laughed and changed the subject without a trace of remorse or care – he just wasn't meant to get that information, at least, not yet.

On the date Joshua had taken her to his favorite place in The Common, a small Victorian shelter out of the way from all of the other good folks that enjoyed the park on a beautiful fall evening.

He had brought mixed sliced deli meat, fresh bread from the local bakery, salad he'd purloined from the school cafeteria and a bottle of his mother's homemade grape juice, non-alcoholic of course, that he had saved for such an occasion as this. He carried it all in a basket with two hand towels and two very nice antique cut glass goblets he'd purchased at a secondhand store for one dollar each.

It was the very best he could do, as a college student, money was not just "tight' it was "non-existent."

For the movie portion of the evening's pleasure, he downloaded *Fantasia* – the Disney classic – onto his iPad. They shared a set of earbuds as they snuggled into a blanket and under the two stars that dared to shine through the overwhelming city glare that obscured all of the others.

That was ten days ago, now he found himself back in the library wondering where his Summer had gone.

And, there she was, far back in the stacks doing what he always saw her doing: replacing the endless stream of books that found their way back onto her cart.

She smiled as she saw Joshua come around the corner. It was a heartfelt kind smile that put all of his fears to rest. It was the first time he realized that she was truly joyful to see him, just as he was to see her.

"Are you ready for your next assignment?" she asked without hesitation.

"Why yes, I do believe I am," answered Joshua with as little surprise as he could possibly muster.

"Then find the ancient text, tucked away with the other treasures; it will be cataloged as the *Scroll Of Wisdom*. I will only ask of you one thing from your sojourn into this particular subject – yet it will be the hardest question you may ever be asked."

Summer smiled, but her eyes told a different story and instantly Joshua knew he'd better be more than brilliant with his response to whatever the question would be. For he knew, that if he didn't get this one perfect, Summer would be a season he'd never enjoy again.

* * * * * * *

"So young Joshua, my question is as follows: What are the basic differences between facts, knowledge, and wisdom?" Summer asked without even a hint of a hello or small talk.

At that exact moment Joshua knew that this question was not new to her, she had been at this stage in a relationship many times before. That salient fact gave him tremendous concern...

"You must answer without stumble or fall – and with few words." Once again she pierced him with the depth of her powder blue eyes that seemed other-worldly.

Employing all he'd learned from his efforts with both courage and light, he stood tall and straight before her and gallantly answered her question. "My dear Summer Rains, facts are an endless stream of observations of that which is around us. The effects of gravity and other physical phenomena would be the perfect examples of such observable events that can be, both replicated and cataloged for future usage as well as passed to the next generation. Knowledge has the created benefit of piecing together facts gleaned into a format as to anticipate a very certain outcome or desired effect."

Joshua took two deep breaths, then he delivered the final portion of the three-part question at hand, "...what is Wisdom?"

"Yet, wisdom is a far different reality. Wisdom deals neither in facts or knowledge, for both of those are mere renderings of man." Taking a third breath, Joshua looked squarely into the eyes that exploded into his very soul, and then delivered his final summation. "Wisdom accounts for all things, not just facts and knowledge, but wisdom deals in truths. Spiritual truths delivered from a divine source that transcends both time and space. Man deals in knowledge, but God deals in truth. And, that alone, is the beginning of wisdom."

Time stopped and a tremendous burden was lifted from the pounding heart beating within Joshua.

Summer set down the books she held in her hands, climbed down the rolling ladder that she always struggled with, took three steps across the divide and taking Joshua's startled cheeks, one in each hand, she gently kissed him on the lips with a kindness of love that had no basis in fact or knowledge.

With that first kiss, Joshua and Summer both knew that he'd not only passed the tests, but that their worlds had been invaded by more than just wisdom.

* * * * * * *

Ten days later he still didn't have Summer's phone number. So when he finally found her, as always, in the furthest reaches of the library struggling with the wayward ladder and standing on her tip toes re-stocking the shelves, obtaining that number was his quest. It was his singular objective.

However, Summer had a different goal in mind. As soon as she saw him with his hands steadying her ladder, she danced down and without saying a word pulled a neatly folded piece of paper from her back pocket and handed it to him with a big smile. She then turned, went right back up the rickety ladder, and resumed her work.

It appeared that Joshua had been dismissed, very politely, but dismissed nonetheless.

He stopped at a desk along a long row of desks, which seemed to stretch to infinity. Joshua looked down to see that at some point in the past a lonely student, in quiet desperation, carved two words into the wooden surface: *SAVE ME...*

Joshua understood the need that simple plea for help commanded.

He pulled the folded paper out of his vest pocket to find what Summer had handed him, with such a kind smile and an elegant dismissal. It was a golden Japanese origami crane folded perfectly – on the one wing hand written in the most elegant calligraphy were two words: *UNFOLD ME...*

So he did.

That is exactly how he found himself, once again, back in the antiquities section of the library under the obnoxious ever present gaze of the woman who stared at his every move.

Once he found the crystal sleeve with the scroll he'd been assigned to find, unfurl, photograph, print and then read aloud three times – as he'd been instructed before – he donned his silk gloves and unrolled the ancient text marked: *Scroll Of Love.* The subject matter startled him as he began his latest assignment with great excitement that obviously the person with the desperate plea for help had carved into the desk was searching for.

* * * * * * *

Between finals and Summer's latest assignment, he'd lost complete track of what day of the week it was. It must be Friday he thought looking at his iPhone calendar to confirm; it was indeed Friday. Two finals, one at 8 a.m. and another at 7 p.m. Who schedules these things?

By the end of the day he felt like his brain was on fire from a forced exodus through the burning hot sands of academia. So he postponed his adventure into Summer's challenge until the following day. Summoning up his courage, dressing as best he could as a Medieval Town Crier, he proceeded to the local mall's food court with a copy of the *Scroll Of Love* tucked under his arm. It was a Saturday at high noon and the place was swarming with noisy customers, all in a state of semi-controlled mayhem.

So with a bold announcement to the lively crowd he proceeded in his quest to play the role he'd been dealt. Reading the *Scroll Of Love* with as much dramatic eloquence as he could speak into the massive hall of dining, he captured his audience; the crowd unexpectedly quieted and intently listened to his announcement of condensed and profound ancient wisdom.

Not only did he receive a standing ovation for his efforts by the noonday gathering of souls, but also one elderly lady with snow-white hair at the Chinese Buffet walked towards him with great effort as she leaned on her cane. Without any words, she gave Joshua the biggest hug of heartfelt thanks he may have ever received, then she spoke life into him. "GOD bless you my son – all will be well."

Tears rolled down her face as she cried like a *little girl lost* who'd finally found her way home after a very long time.

SUMMER RAINS

* * * * * * *

Nothing he had ever encountered had prepared him for the hug from the elderly lady at the food court. Joshua could not remove the depth of the experience from of his mind. It rolled around in the furthest reaches of his psyche, then it would burst forth at the strangest times; while in the shower, walking to class, looking for Summer Rains– who it appeared - couldn't be found.

Then he finally had the deepest thought that put his quandary at ease: *The brevity of life is astounding and should never be ignored.* As soon as he synthesized that thought, he could finally, after weeks of pondering, put the matter to rest.

Joshua lingered over small sips of the world's finest hot cocoa at the Chocolatier's tiny table. It was at the base of *Candy Mountain* where Summer Rains lived.

All through winter break she never appeared and Joshua had never felt more alone, even after visiting his small town and family for Christmas. He returned in the hope of watching the New Year's fireworks with Summer Rains; they were impressive, but strange to watch alone and without her by his side.

So he lingered at the wire mesh table hoping to find his girl with the powder blue eyes.

But it appeared that the warmth of summer had disappeared and the loneliness of winter had invaded all things...

Chapter Six

Surreal beauty was the only possible description of the liquid world where he dwelled. Cascading with visual bounty, the barber pole shrimp extended family was cleaning a wrasse that knew exactly where to come for such a needed breath of freedom from the tiny particles that it couldn't reach or scrape away via its own efforts. To his left a huge coral head held an entire colony of domino fish that created their own little flurry of activity much like the shrimp at his feet. One rogue octopus who went skittering by looking for lunch saw Joshua and did an abrupt hairpin turn in mid-ocean flight; it then disappeared around the corner of the reef in a flagrant display of colors rippling across it's highly textured skin.

Waves continued to force themselves against the pinnacles above, exploding into foaming masses like white clouds, pushing as far down into the tranquility of the crystal blue lagoon as they possibly could.

Out of the chaos, once again the pack of ulua appeared, this time from the exact opposite edge of the foaming tempests of rolling thunder. They were looking for more fish to shred and protein to consume.

Huge cathedrals and pillars of light walked to and fro – appearing and then evaporating - as the liquid dance above allowed.

Joshua looked at his gauges with disinterest. Doing the math, he had sixteen minutes remaining. But with the new flight path of the squadron of hungry ulua being on rampant display, he now knew one more direction not to go.

28

His choices were narrowing, much like his timeline to make a decision.

* * * * * *

Finally, the owner of The Chocolatier couldn't put off his curiosity any longer. Wiping his sugar coated hands on his white apron, he appraised Joshua with a fatherly look and a knowing smile. "I assume you are waiting for beautiful young lady that lives high above our humble store?"

It was not really posed as a question.

"You know Summer Rains?" Joshua was a little more than shocked at the question posed so accurately.

"Everyone here knows young Miss Rains, she is our joy and delight when her smile enters our world." The owner spoke with unbridled enthusiasm.

"Is there any way to get in touch with her? I haven't been able to reach her since Christmas break, and I've finished the assignment she gave me." Joshua half blurted out, not able to contain himself with his desire to speak of his favorite subject.

"Mr. and Mrs. Rains, Summer's parents, have been customers of ours since the very first day we opened this store. In fact, I have an order almost ready for delivery to their estate. Would you care to deliver it for us? It will take but a few more minutes for me to prepare." The candy maker knew the answer before he ever posed the question.

"Yes, I will wait, sir." Joshua almost exploded with his instant acquiescence to the task being offered.

When the candy maker returned to his shop, his loving wife laughingly observed, "So the Rains family needs a delivery of an order they never made?"

"No! That young man needs to deliver a message he knows not how to create. Shall we help in his pursuit of love, or must I do this alone?" He raised one eyebrow to his loving wife.

"Well, they do seem to love the dark chocolate covered blueberries..."

* * * * * * *

Joshua pulled into the Rains Estate in his high mileage Honda Civic with dings and patches of various colors on every possible panel and corner. The four tires, worn and threadbare, were of four different brands and three different sizes, creating the effect of pulling hard left when braking and drifting wide right when not. Over two hundred thousand miles of long distance commutes on poorly maintained roads had brought him to the estate. It was like docking a battered dingy alongside a super yacht, it was beyond out-of-place, it was borderline shameful.

Yet Joshua was so excited he didn't even notice the strange juxtaposition or the obvious irony of the event unfolding. This was where Summer Rains lived! That fact alone was enough to look past the obvious. So he gathered up The Chocolatier fancy box of delights, in an even fancier bag and proceeded to deliver the order that had never been made.

* * * * * * *

Joshua instinctively took off his shoes as he entered the Rains' mansion. It sat majestic and high above the sand dunes overlooking the wind tossed Atlantic Ocean, which exploded against the shoreline without remorse or excuse.

Padding along in his socks on blue gum eucalyptus floors, it was impossible not to notice the incredible displays of wealth all around. Fine inlaid furniture from a bygone era held knick-knacks of beautiful handmade koa boxes and Grecian statues both large and delicate. It was overwhelming his senses as all things were polished to the highest sheen. Not a speck of dust invaded the space that had small spotlights accentuating every piece of artwork, making them standout one from another.

Joshua stood stunned amazed before a Matisse oil painting, this hallway was more impressive than any museum he'd ever been in! Off to the side, a bookcase held dozens of rocks and minerals – many that glowed fluorescent – others that sparkled of gems. Gold nuggets and strands encapsulated in quartz sat beside their cousins of platinum and copper, jade and emerald, ruby and diamond.

Long oval antique crystal chandeliers, perfect in their form, lit the hallway overhead to complete the substance of being thrust beyond anything he'd ever seen or imagined. As the hallway split both to the left and to the right, Joshua followed the little girl who'd allowed him to enter, motioning for him to follow. As she giggled and slid down the hallways, he did his best to keep up while trying to take it all in. She had never introduced herself; she just smiled at the door after seeing the bag he held in his hands from The Chocolatier, and said very elegantly, well beyond her years, "Please follow me, sir."

So he did.

Now he found himself in the depths of a world he'd only ever heard about. He'd heard about wealth of this caliber, but certainly had never known it up close and personal.

He was from Appalachia, and what he was experiencing within this mansion was certainly not doublewide trailers, broken down cars, and shattered dreams.

Following the young girl to the final turn, deep within the mansion's extravagant corridors, she announced to the man poring over maps in the corner, well lit by the two-story set of glass windows overlooking the courtyard and the driveway where Joshua had parked: "Father, we have a delivery. It appears to be from Mother's favorite shop in the whole-wide-world!" Then the child, who was maybe twelve years old, turned and smiled at Joshua. Then without a care in the world she sped back down the corridors, skipping and sliding to points unknown.

Yet, not before he caught the color of her eyes; they were the same joyous powder blue as Summer's eyes. Obviously they were sisters. That simple fact dawned on him as she dropped him in this sanctum, with the paneled walls and priceless artifacts all around.

Mr. Rains looked once again at the car in the driveway, laughed a gentle laugh, and then turned toward the gangly young man holding the bag of chocolates. Joshua was quivering a bit from all he'd encountered along the way. Mr. Rains, standing in the home office of his family's empire, took two steps across the great divide and reached out to shake Joshua's hand with a grip of steel as he received the bag with his other.

Setting The Chocolatier's candy treasures on his neatly stacked desk, he looked inside. Smiling, he said, "Summer's mother will love these, they are her very favorite." Then, not missing a beat, he added, "But then you wouldn't know that because you aren't an employee of the Goldsteins who own the shop, are you?"

It was not a question. Mr. Rains raised a knowing eyebrow and looked at the stunned young man before him who obviously had an ulterior objective.

"No, sir. They sent me it appears, on a mission-of-mercy to find Summer. Every evening I would sit on their veranda sipping a cup of hot cocoa waiting for Summer to come back to her place in the city. It has come to the point that I've become worried for her, sir."

Joshua was doing his best to employ every ounce of courage he possessed. "Also, I think they were showing compassion on me, their hot chocolate is very expensive and I was down to paying for it in pennies."

Mr. Rains laughed a hearty laugh. "Here, look at this map young man and tell me what you think." With that, he opened up his world and his family to the scrawny college student with the completely transparent and honest disposition.

And thus, Joshua's journey into a world he'd never known began...

* * * * * * *

It is a well-known fact that making three deeply flawed decisions in a row often leads to tragedy.

Most fatal accidents can be traced back to their root cause as a string of poor decisions, one stacked upon another. Rarely is just one bad decision, or poor choice, enough to cause a fatality. Through the eons of time concerning human endeavor, it most likely takes at least three.

Joshua sitting at the bottom of the ocean - with the surface in total chaos while sitting in a sea of tranquility - had made two. He did not wish to make the third, so he continued to sit while pondering his options. All as the minutes firmly passed by...

Chapter Seven

"So you are here for my oldest daughter, Summer?" Mr Rains posed this as a question, but it did not need an answer as it was so obvious.

"Yes, Mr. Rains, I suppose I am." Joshua still totally taken aback by the awesome collection of wealth, culture, and refinement on vivid display all around him. It wasn't just the artwork or sculptures, or the three-story mansion of stone and glass. Or the grounds, which even in the snow and ice, were stunning to the senses.

It was the quiet elegance of the family that resided here and called this place their "home".

"You know, young man, that Summer is a challenge of biblical proportions, more of a season than even her name implies. Summer is one of my greatest joys. She is *precious cargo* in my world. She is full of nuance and even more than a touch of mystery, her genius has been on vivid display since she was very very young."

Mr. Rains looked intently at the stalwart young man who was just now starting to squirm. But it also appeared that a deep-seated courage was emerging as well, so he continued with his introduction to his perspective on his wondrous daughter. "As a case in point, when she was four years old we took her to the Metropolitan Museum of Art in the city and walked her through the works of the masters: Van Gogh, Dali, Michelangelo, Raphael – all of the great artists of their eras. She stopped before an obscure painting on loan from a traveling Russian exhibition. She was mesmerized by an oil painting by a rather unknown painter. Finally, I asked her, 'Summer what do you see, darling, that is so important?' With tremendous observational skills - so far beyond her age - she answered, 'Daddy, the artist is so lonely.'"

Time stood frozen in the office where Mr. Rains and Joshua stood; they both pondered the profoundness of the answer given by a four year old child.

"Are you truly ready for such a challenge, such a quirky genius, such an outrageous adventure as my daughter - whom I love immensely?" Mr. Rains asked, already knowing the answer once again.

After a tremendous pause...

"Only with your permission and help, sir." Joshua then added, "It appears that I will need all of the help I can possibly muster, and Mr. Rains, the help I'll need is yours."

They looked at each other, nodded and looked down at the tilted table with the map clipped to it to study the project at hand. Both knew the map had virtually nothing to do with Joshua's pursuit of Summer.

* * * * * * *

As they looked at a map of Tonopah, Nevada Mr. Rains started giving a short dissertation on what they were actually looking for; it wasn't the beauty or extraordinary quality of the high-resolution full spectral satellite image. It was the information contained and exact details to be gleaned from the large print before them.

Pointing at the map, at various points contained within it, Mr. Rains offered, "I've been told this is the most valuable dirt in all of North America. Back in the day, just after the end of WWII, there were a group of test pilots working on the next generation of fighter aircraft for the Air Force. Everything was, of course, top secret. Those pilots were no ordinary men and eventually would become the basis for the American Space

Program, or what we today know as NASA. However, I am getting ahead of the story. I had the immense pleasure of knowing one of the original test pilots of that bygone era in American history. He told me, 'Every day at the crack-of-dawn we would be performing test flights in the early morning air over a certain section of the high-altitude desert. Over that particular section, exactly as the sun broke the horizon, a certain portion would flash pure gold. That flash reminded us of the phenomena we'd experienced while flying missions during the war in the Deep South Pacific at sunset. That event was, and still is, known as a *Green Flash*. It is the briefest of events, but if you are ready to observe, it is unmistakable.'"

"I see that the area is known as Goldfields, sir." Joshua pointed at the map key imprinted in the corner of the 3 feet by 4 feet map. He smiled as he made the obvious leap in logic. "It appears that the elderly man and his cohorts must have discovered something."

Mr. Rains liked this young man and was starting to see a glimmer of why his daughter was taking the time to reel him in. "Yes they did. Indeed, they found more than they had ever imagined, more than they ever dreamed of. For a chosen few that knowledge would lead to untold wealth, for all of the others – that is the ones that survived their day job of breaking the sound barrier – the information was even deadlier than hurling through the atmosphere at wicked speeds in frail machines made by man."

Joshua, with eyes wide open asked his stupidest question of the day. "Is this how you have become so rich?" He swept his arms around the walnut paneled office with the huge windows overlooking the estate's manicured gardens as the silent snow fell.

Mr. Rains looked at him with a look that only a seasoned warrior could give a wayward naive apprentice. "Come back in exactly one week, at which time you will give me a short version of the basic difference between being rich and being wealthy. Thank you for the chocolates, I'll be sure to let Summer know that you have made it this far."

With that assignment, Joshua found himself being both stunned and summarily dismissed.

On his way back to campus, while maneuvering through the traffic and congestion, he realized that the Rains family was full of surprises, and that with Summer the fruit did not fall too far from the tree.

* * * * * * * *

Braving the snow that persisted relentlessly, exactly one week to the minute, Joshua showed up at the Rains Estate full of trepidation.

"What have you discovered about the differences between being rich and being wealthy young man?" asked Mr. Rains after he turned around from the very animated phone conversation he was just finishing, all as Joshua was delivered to his office threshold, by the effervescent young lady, who refused to engage in any type of conversation. She just giggled, danced, slid and skipped along the polished hallways. Then, as before, she simply disappeared back into the depths of the pretentious mansion abode.

"Sir, every time I thought I was on the trail of a definitive difference – the storyline, the information, and the very definition I sought – it would all unravel with overlapping facts that would confuse the issue. After a week of one of the most in-depth studies I have ever tried to complete, I stand before you unable to answer your simple question, and with that I am afraid that I have left you down." Worried lines of confusion wrinkled Joshua's youthful face. With his head down and completely at a loss, he felt far out of his element.

Mr. Rains appraised the young man before him. He then stood and walked over to his favorite section of his office where he kept his maps. Turning he looked at Joshua and answered his own question that had bewildered Joshua to no end. "All that you see around you, all of these things are of man. That well-worn Honda you drive, this estate along with the art and sculptures we've been blessed to acquire through the course of the decades which give our home character and ambiance. These maps and the assets they represent scattered from Chile to Madagascar are just the riches of man. But that smile on my youngest daughter's face, her easy laugh, the light in her eyes – that is wealth. Riches are the things of the earth, wealth are the gifts of heaven."

After a very intense pause - that seemed to extend for days - Mr. Rains added a final declaration: "Wealth is not who loves you – but why they love you."

Allowing the wisdom to be absorbed, Mr. Rains eventually turned back to his tilted map table. He then picked up the conversation were they had left off during Joshua's last visit. Stunned, Joshua contemplated the ramifications of the answer he had so diligently sought.

"Those test pilots, extraordinary souls that they were, eventually took the time and efforts to seek out the source of the phenomena that they had started calling *The Gold Illusion*. Little did they know how deadly accurate of a nickname that it would prove to be." When Mr. Rains said that he raised an eyebrow to Joshua as a signal to really pay close attention.

"You see, those men were skilled, capable, battle hardened, and tested. Many of them were survivors of intense military campaigns across three continents. They were unprepared for the riches of the world they would discover here." As he pointed to the Caldera section of the map with his index finger, he said, "And that unpreparedness for this new type of battlefield they encountered would eventually kill all but one of them."

Mr. Rains looked intently at his young audience of one, and finished his thoughts. "One survivor out of ten very brilliant and extraordinary men. That, young Mr. Joshua is a deathtrap with a very pronounced kill ratio."

"So what killed them?" Joshua was profoundly intrigued by the story.

"The consumption of riches. For they found exactly what they were looking for. Goldfields had unmatched quantities of gold rich ore scattered as dust all across the surface of this area. Vast quantities of gold dust, platinum, rhodium, and other precious elements were discovered as easy pickings, especially within the Calderas. Every single one of them became multi-millionaires literally overnight. Back in the late forties, that was immense amounts of liquidity and riches." Mr. Rains leaned against a polished walnut table, sipped his coffee, and then continued. "That instant access to man's riches destroyed them. Alcohol, failed marriages, contraband and many other bad habits devastated each of them as those wicked proclivities and vices became more and more pronounced in their lives.

"You see, with large sums of money, they each had finally acquired the means to unleash their deepest proclivities and held-back desires. Shattered dreams. Destroyed lives. Failed marriages. Abandoned children. The curses of being rich destroyed them."

"Mr. Rains, you said one survived the trap, how on earth did he escape? How did he beat the overwhelming odds?"

"There you are! The young man my Summer speaks very highly of." Mr. Rains laughed a gentle laugh as he went on. "At first, like the others, he gave in to his darkest desires. But, in a bout of drunken meanness he saw the danger he'd become in the reflections and depths of the eyes of the only person he ever loved more than himself – his childhood sweetheart. So he put his addictions aside, embraced love over vice, and then he found his way to an altar, sought forgiveness of our LORD who knows no boundaries when it comes to grace. And with that transformation of divine intervention, the tenth man lived. He is now over ninety years young and has homes and villas all over the world, children in the halls of power far and wide. He lives on the slopes of the Andes and walks his vineyard as he is able."

Joshua offered in stunned amazement, "You know this man, one of the original founders of Goldfields?"

"Yes I do, and, GOD willing maybe someday you will too." Mr. Rains, not quite being done with the lesson at hand and the exact point he wished to instill on the young fellow standing with him. "The difference between man's riches and GOD's wealth is the difference between shattered dreams and promises kept."

Snow fell on the manicured estate outside the window; it also covered the multi-colored beaten Honda. It appeared that snow knew no boundaries when it came to the difference between exquisite and affordable.

Finally, Joshua asked the question he'd wished to have asked during his prior visit. "Where's Summer?" He did not need to include how much he missed her, that information was glaringly obvious behind his words.

"She's in Chile, with her mother. They're at that villa sitting against the base of the Andes visiting her grandfather." Then adding slyly, "It may be winter here in the northern hemisphere, but it is Summer wherever she is."

That brought a joyous smile to both of their faces.

"Next week, same time, same place? Your next assignment is: What is the most valuable asset you will ever own? As a hint, it is a one-word answer."

This time Mr. Rains took the time and effort to walk Joshua to the door, past the artwork and antiquities, Joshua smiled and forlornly shook his mentor's hand, then he braved the cold of the north while dreaming of Summer's warmth hidden away so far to the south...

* * * * * * *

Only the depth of his awareness had changed as time spent on the bottom of the lagoon permeated all around. With the thunderous waves above, the ulua were doing their best to decimate the schools of bait fish that changed shapes to absorb their bombardments of serrated teeth and jaws of death. Barber pole shrimp were preening the next fish in line. The domino fish were doing whatever it is that such cute fish do. Soon he'd have to take action, for time was no longer on his side. And, if there was anything he'd learned, doing nothing was also a choice and rarely offered a positive outcome.

Chapter Eight

With massive powder blue eyes of joyous wonder, the family trait, Summer's younger sister met Joshua at the door. Skipping and sliding, as she always did, she led him to his appointment with her father in his office den.

"Father! Summer's young gentleman is here to see you again." With that elegant announcement, delivered both with enthusiasm and carefree intent, as only a twelve year old could, she disappeared around the corner to points unknown.

Spinning in his Corinthian leather chair, tooled and tucked with brass tacks, Mr. Rains put down his precision writing instrument and looked up with a smile to greet his young apprentice.

"So, Joshua, what have you arrived at? What is the most valuable asset you will ever own?" Then very seriously, "there is only one correct answer."

"Well, sir, I researched and read. After our last meeting, I knew it couldn't be possible for it to be a work of art, for even a masterpiece of museum quality is not of inherent wealth. And, after even deeper contemplation, I had to rule out family and friends. For, unlike things, they cannot ever be owned." Joshua, taking a deep breath, chose his next words wisely. "Sir, the best I can ascertain, the very best answer I can possibly muster in a single word is...*time*."

"Excellent! Once again, young Joshua, you continue to make me smile. Well done." Mr. Rains was more than pleased with the answer.

Joshua sighed in relief and managed to find a chair to sit in.

"Now let us talk about time. Your most valuable asset you will ever own. Funny, it is an asset with no definable value and you will never know how much will ever be remaining in your life's personal hourglass.

"Time is the measuring device for how you value yourself and how you value those around you. You see I know people who place virtually a zero valuation on their time, or their efforts on their fields of knowledge and expertise. For them, spending time working for others and being on their schedule is "just how it is." Mr. Rains shook his head in awe. "They squander their most precious gift from GOD and waste it away waiting for others to make decisions for them. It is beyond sad, but yet, so common as to barely be worthy of mention."

Mr. Rains walked around his desk and joined Joshua in the chair beside him as a means to make his next point very sincerely. "Others spend so much time on themselves and their pursuits that they neglect those around them. Eventually they become isolated as those family members, friends, and loved ones become no more than faded memories and dreams deferred. They too, in their daily choices of time management, choose poorly. They die as lonely souls at the end of a life spent sprinting across a barren desert devoid of love and intimacy.

"Every day you must choose: What shall I do today? With that choice, that simple decision of time management, it will determine what type of life you shall acquire. Will you gain a life of joy and happiness, wealth and wisdom, laughter and love? Or, will you be hassled by others and their demands and eventually herded into a corral not of your making?"

Joshua nodded his head in agreement; such a simple delivery on such a complex concept. For the first time in his life he realized he had, at many points in his short life, failed the test of time. Yet with this new knowledge, he could apply wisdom to the equation and do better – he immediately grasped the concept and how it applied to him on a very personal level.

Mr. Rains rose to not so subtly announce that this meeting was completed, with that, ever the diligent mentor, he posed the next question of his not so hidden agenda of bettering the life of the youngster who had dreams of his daughter. "What exactly is the wisdom of wealth?"

With the micro-expression that burst within Joshua's eyes, Mr. Rains knew he'd hit a homerun with this particular challenge. He was truly excited to see how Joshua would respond.

At the door, Mr. Rains parted ways with Joshua. "Next week, same time, will that be alright with you?"

"I will be here, sir. Thank you for your precious time, Mr. Rains, I greatly appreciate you sharing your most valuable asset with me."

* * * * * * *

Sitting up in bed in the middle of the night he had an absolute epiphany of biblical proportions. He'd been pondering Mr. Rains' latest question and any and all answers he'd tried to work through were inferior at best. Then, at exactly 3:33 a.m., on a dark winter's night, when even his dorm room that he was cocooned within was silent, he'd discovered the key. That epiphany had made him sit bolt upright in bed with the answer he so desperately sought.

It was divinely brilliant timing since the very next day was his weekly session with Mr. Rains.

SUMMER RAINS

* * * * * * *

Mr. Rains set straight up in his chair, startled by the answer Joshua delivered to him. "So, would you be kind enough to give me that answer one more time, Joshua? I wish to make sure that I fully grasp it in its totality."

"Yes, sir. I will do my best. Time is our most valuable asset, fleeting and unknown as it may be. Wealth allows us to acquire more time, for wealth is freedom: Freedom to pursue our very own passions and dreams. Freedom to spend time with our loved ones. Freedom of motion. Freedom to have the ability to travel. Freedom enough to dream. And, if you will, even the freedom to chase those dreams no matter where they lead. And should wealth be obtained in large enough quantities, no matter the duration or costs of those pursuits. Therefore, in summation, sir: *The wisdom of wealth is that it buys time."*

The handmade curly koa clock ticked slowly by as it sat on the highest shelf of the bookcase. Its precisely punctuated tics broke the otherwise dead silence filling the room.

"That may be the single best answer to that question I've ever heard. Bravo young Joshua. You are on the road to wisdom." Mr. Rains nodded his head in fatherly approval.

"While we are on the subject of time, would you do me, the entire Rains family, the honor of staying for supper? Summer and her mother are supposed to land about now and should be here shortly." Mr. Rains posed the question knowing what the answer will be.

With greatly exaggerated agreement, Joshua's day had become tremendously better. Little did he know, that with the advent of the Rains homecoming, his journey to knowledge, wisdom, and acceptance was about to become way more interestingly complex. The lessons that Mr. Rains so willing shared were about to become mere footnotes to that which lay in store for him. Because now Joshua would be thrust into a world that included Summer's mother.

And mothers care little about the creation of wealth and the intricacies of time management. Mothers care about the mysteries of life, the intentions of the heart, and the depths of love one soul has towards another.

Joshua was about to find out, that just like Summer, Mrs. Rains had a way of stripping away all agendas and lying bare the truth.

* * * * * * *

Watching his bubbles rise towards the surface to join the thunderous waves above, he realized that shortly it would be time to make a decision. He had to make some type of move to regain the freedom of an exit from this wonderland of liquid turquoise joy he was immersed within. With that salient fact, he took three kicks up; maybe a change of perspective would clarify his next course of action.

If nothing else, it would extend his bottom time, and with those three kicks to a new depth of 45 feet, he bought himself some time.

And time, as Joshua well knew, was all he had...

Chapter Nine

Hovering at 45 feet depth, Joshua knew that this was far enough. He could feel the downbursts of the horrendous surf exploding above and the first glimmers of current pressing against his wetsuit and fins.

Where on earth was his dive partner? As they entered the water from the protected pebble beach, his dive partner said, "We'll get some lobsters and fish for dinner, it's going to be great." Twenty minutes later, his dive partner - Summer's long lost cousin - had vanished. He was there one second, and then Joshua took a mini-side venture into a small ravine looking for something to spear in the cracks along the bottom, when he turned around his new found friend was gone! Joshua was alone without a shred of a clue of how he'd gotten so lost.

First major mistake was he didn't dial in his compass. Second compounded mistake was he didn't stay glued to the only person that knew the spot well enough to survive on a day like this. Third potentially catastrophic mistake remained uncertain...

Taking a good look around, he kept the facts he'd gleaned clearly in the forefront of his mind. As the ulua probably emerge from the open ocean - do not go there. Up would be disastrous at best. Three other directions – left, right, and straight – all looked the same from here...

Where was his dive partner?

Hovering he conserved his air, controlled his breathing, and did his best to enjoy the magnitude of the beauty that enabled him to transcend the experience. No wonder they called this isolated pristine haven, this ocean wonderland, Heaven's Threshold...

* * * * * *

"I see you met my father and little sister," Summer offered with a quirky smile as Joshua helped unload the groceries from the car and carry them to the pantry. "I heard that you've been spending time here while I've been gone." Summer smiled when she said it, she gave the comment as a statement of fact with a bit of knowing laughter.

Joshua could barely respond as the girls, Mrs. Rains, Summer, and her little sister all loaded him to the max with the heaviest items of canned goods, fruits, and drinks.

"Your father has been taking the time to teach me many things. He has a strange way of getting me to grasp how the world operates," Joshua said with strained breath as the trio herded him to the pantry once again.

"Much like his oldest daughter..." Summer left the remark hang in the air rather mischievously.

"Yes. Much like the girl that abandoned me to drink hot chocolate and discover, on my own, where she'd gone." Joshua's response included more than a touch of *snark,* as he was rather proud of his exploits.

"Thank you gallant sir for finding me. I am glad it took effort, otherwise it would have been of very little value," Summer responded with dancing eyes.

Joshua melted.

Mrs. Rains interfered with their reveries. "Joshua, would you be kind enough to help me in the kitchen? It has been a long time since we've had a home cooked meal. Santiago is a half a world away, and I need real nourishment to replenish my soul. I think we all do."

Joshua's acquiescence was immediate. Whatever Mrs. Rains wanted was instantly his deepest desire to accomplish.

Little did he know he was in for the most subtly skilled grilling of his life, and without notice, the grilling was to start immediately.

"So, Joshua, you met our Summer in the library?"

"Yes, Mrs. Rains, I did." He answered, unaware of a mother's subtle agenda being implemented one nuance at a time. He was hopelessly oblivious and had not a shred of concern about the series of questions coming his way.

"I've heard that you took my daughter on a date in the park ..."

"Yes, dinner and a movie." Joshua perked up. He had not been aware that he'd been the topic of conversation somewhere along the way.

"So, what type of movie was your choice for such an evening out?" She struggled to reach the olive oil, just out of reach in the pantry. When she reached high and fumbled with the tips of her fingers, she reminded Joshua of Summer struggling with the decrepit ladder in the furthest reaches of the library. Joshua immediately reached past her and retrieved the olive oil for Mrs. Rains. She smiled at him and checked 'observant and helpful' off of her internal motherly checklist – a checklist which was vast.

"We watched *Fantasia,* the dancing hippos scene always makes me laugh."

Mrs. Rains checked off 'appropriate' on her checklist, maybe even 'wholesome' which was even better. Mrs. Rains absorbed the information, realizing that this young man had class enough to show her precious daughter a gloriously timeless classic that didn't include any vulgar or inappropriate behavior.

"So, young Mr. Joshua, what brings you true joy?" Mrs. Rains started with one of her real questions as she handed him an onion and nodded at the cutting board with an ultra-sharp Japanese MAC knife on it.

"Chopped or diced?" he asked.

"Diced will be better." She checked one more not so minor item off of her internal checklist; he appeared to be nuanced to detail.

"I guess simple things bring me true joy, like this. Being in the kitchen with my mum and having dad sitting at the counter sipping coffee and making stray comments."

"Do you help your mother with her cooking?" Mrs. Rains carried on with her line of questioning while she prepared a Greek salad with both skilled hands and a soft elegance.

"I never did much before. I'd sit with my dad at the counter and mostly observe. But now, since I've been gone from home for over three years, I love to get involved and help her cook. I even help her bake now and again. Funny, I never did before, yet to answer your question, I seem to feel the greatest joy by getting directly involved." Joshua put the extremely sharp knife down, got a far away look deep in his eyes and softly went on, "I miss it so much that when I'm there I wish to completely immerse myself in the process..."

Mrs. Rains absorbed the answer, wiped her hands on her apron with the hand-stitched Andes Mountains on it, reached across the quartz-topped island and held out her hand. Joshua took a step closer and took her hand in his. She looked him directly in the eyes with her brown eyes of brilliance that flashed golden specks as she honestly stated, "Joshua, please call me Grace, I'm so happy that our daughter found you."

With that acknowledgment of inclusion, the awkwardness that permeated the air began to melt and the clinically cold kitchen breathed a divine breath and longing sigh of much needed warmth into Joshua's homesick soul.

* * * * * * *

Lingering at 45 feet in depth, as best as he could, he watched his depth gauge dance between 38 and 60 from the ever present ocean tempests, now way closer than comfortable, exploding in rolling chaotic liquid thunder just above. Trying his very best to visualize the map, once again, of this tiny speck of land in the middle of the huge Pacific Ocean, he reached for his compass to see if its dial would reveal which way he should go.

Nothing! He couldn't envision the island's map and the compass gave him only frustration; it tried to steal the joy of the moment. From his newfound perspective, Joshua realized that the small lagoon was considerably larger than he'd ever imagined.

It became flagrantly apparent that Heaven's Threshold was not just mesmerizingly gorgeous – but it was vast just like the ocean it rested within. Pinnacles and archways, standing resolute and numerous, they overlapped and stood as peaks of sharp black remnants of the island having been created without regard for the needs of man.

He had gained a bit of time and the additional breaths that came with it, but with this new reality, his air reserve was no longer his biggest problem. His most pressing problem appeared to be the vastness of blue space that flowed out all around...

Chapter Ten

Spring semester started in the dead of a brutal cold New England winter that was relentless. All things were frozen and forlorn and, at least for Joshua, as lonely as ever.

Since their family meal at the Rains Estate, he'd not seen or heard a single peep from Summer. Gazing out the window he knew that it would be a while for the city to feel the warmth of a much needed change of seasons.

Joshua was completely consumed by his final semester as a student in quest of an undergraduate degree. What completely baffled him was: Why? The more he engaged in the world's version of a quest for knowledge, the more he realized that there was virtually zero wisdom encapsulated within that journey. Yet, he was a creature of habit and he'd made promises to his parents that needed to be fulfilled. What for? And why? Lingered at the edge of his perception every waking moment. Duty overrode all of those deep-seated ponderings, so he soldiered on regardless of his angst for the tasks at hand.

With this semester's nineteen credits, he was in danger of graduating from these hallowed halls of Harvard's Ivy League undergraduate program. Graduate to what! How would he make a living post-graduation? Constantly that singular question rolled around as a form of unidentifiable concern on the edges of his mind, this lingering doubt really troubled him.

Yet, one overriding need transcended all of that: Where was Summer? Why on earth did he not spot her on his many trips to the library?

So, on his own initiative, he braved the sacred documents room and the vulture of a custodian that tended to dissect his every move, and went into the recesses of that well-lit hidden room in the back of the library complex. Joshua asked to see the *Scroll Of Joy*. With the least joy ever displayed by a person still living, the wrinkled cadaver handed him a crystal sleeve with an ancient parchment rolled tightly within.

Donning the silk gloves, Joshua quietly freed the parchment manuscript from the confines it had inhabited for who knows how long. Employing his three step process: photograph, correlate, and translate – he had the most ancient wisdom readily available to read at his leisure.

No time like the present. So in the presence of his overlord wrinkled librarian curator, he read the *Scroll Of Joy* out loud with great enthusiasm and in his most accomplished and robust voice. As he read the words, the librarian right across from him quivered. After reading the text with complete attention to nuanced emphasis and detail, he gently rolled the parchment and carefully slid it back into the crystal sleeve and handed it back to the stricken woman before him. Then, out of nowhere, he smiled and hugged her! With that unscripted gift of kindness, he startled her with a loud proclamation of immense intensity: "EMBRACE THE JOY!"

Joshua released her and raced past the Guttenberg Bible, leaving the confines of the library to find Summer.

He did not take the time to see the glistening tears of immense release flowing freely down the librarians' rosy cheeks, or the joyous expression bursting forth from the librarian's face that he'd helped to unshackle from years of darkness with a single heartfelt hug. Sometimes a single act of kindness is all it takes.

* * * * * * *

Two days later it dawned on him that he had read a passage in a wayward novel that his mother had given him years earlier. A passage intrigued him from that rarest book on the face of the earth, because there was only one known manuscript in the public domain. It resided in an obscure section, the Heritage Collection, of a public library near his hometown. How it got there he would never know. But someone had the fortitude to make it available as an eBook. So with his limited funds he downloaded it to see if his memory was correct. It was! He found what he sought, it had been written as an introduction given by a young man in front of the world stage to the love interest of his life, the young lady that had captured his heart without ever saying a word. In that epic series called *Rain Falling On Bells*, the re-awakened passage he had sought out was called *I Choose Joy!* As he read it anew, he realized that he liked that rendering of what it meant to embrace joy much better. Having it read to him by his mother helped immensely. For him it was better than the ancient scroll he'd found hidden in the alcoves of the library. They were very similar, but he preferred the newer version. How strange to see an ancient bit of wisdom dovetailing with what should be a modern classic, yet was hidden away for few to find. He decided to keep the newer version readily available should he ever need a reminder of the better path along life's broken trails of triumphs and disasters. His search for joy had been prompted by something that still resonated with him from his time in the kitchen with Mrs. Rains a few weeks back. It was an offhanded remark said with a soft clarity that was hard to miss: "Joshua, there will be no coincidences in your life, only opportunities embraced or vanquished, for all things work together for the glory of our FATHER in heaven. Never forget to embrace joy at every turn."

* * * * * * *

Spring was in the air and Summer was finally back by his side. Although classes were consuming all of his time, he could find an hour, or so, for a touch of Summer Rains' companionship of laughter and lighthearted banter. They would meet at the base of *Candy Mountain* at The Chocolatier and sip hot cocoa seated at the wire mesh outdoor tables. The owner's wife always made them pay, but if it were to be the owner himself, a bill would never arrive at the table.

He chocked it up to *amore*.

Finally, just as spring was relenting in the city of the deep chill, Summer gave Joshua his last challenge. It concerned the innermost secrets of the cavernous library in the heart of academia.

"Find for me, if you dare, the *Scroll Of Love*. Let's see what the ancients had to say about the oldest known vibration that holds the very fabric of creation together. Bring the captured text to me and we'll decrypt it together."

Summer looked at him with her massive powder blue eyes that shown with fires of mystery. She added, "That is only if you dare."

Within seconds Joshua had his *Nikes* on and was jogging fast towards the bridge over the Charles River. He headed back to campus and into the depths of the corridors of man's knowledge. Yet hiding amongst those endless books were to be found bits, pieces and shreds of wisdom contained in hidden and secret places.

* * * * * * *

The librarian's demeanor was completely different. The countenance of her face shone with joy and her drab faded gray 'schoolmarm' clothes, she'd worn for oh-so-long, had been exchanged for color and a vibrancy that she hadn't embraced for decades, much like the light shining within her eyes. When Joshua saw her he could hardly believe she was the same human being who had petrified him for months.

Her smile lit the way as she pranced along to the sacred room with the ancient texts. "Young Joshua, how may I be honored to help you in your search for wisdom today?"

He could not get over the dramatic change standing so elegantly before him, but decided to seize the moment. "Well..." opening up with information he'd never have shared in her previous hostile condition, "My girl, Miss Summer Rains, has sent me on a quest. She would like for me to retrieve the *Scroll Of Love* so we can ponder its wisdom together. Would you be kind enough to help me find that particular manuscript?" Joshua spoke with a wonderful smile; it seemed that good moods were immediately infectious.

Her expression completely changed; she became sullen giving the news that pierced her at the deepest levels, Since she was a keeper of documents, it pained her at an esoteric level to have to tell Joshua: "I am incredibly sorry, but that was one of the only texts destroyed when the treasury was recovered from the underwater Blue Room Cavern. It has been damaged virtually beyond any hope of recovery. Only fragments remain from that priceless artifact, and those bits, pieces and shreds of remnants have been shipped to Israel where forensics masters are working on whatever recovery can be accomplished. They are the same expert teams that worked on the *Dead Sea Scrolls*. It may take decades before even the tiniest renderings are available for us to enjoy and ponder."

But then she brightened, and said with vigor he didn't know she could possess, "Follow me young man, for I do not know how or who captured that information, but back in the late seventies that scroll, I believe, was written into an obscure book called *Fragments Of Truths*. How appropriate."

With that book properly checked out and in hand, and with a newfound vigor of his own, Joshua proceeded to run like the wind back across the river to share his unexpected adventure and glorious 'find' with the first girl he'd ever loved. It was really strange to think of any girl in a way that made his heart race, just as his feet did as he continued to run back to Summer.

The librarian knew she may never again see this young man who had been able to breathe hope back into her world, for she knew deep down he would be lost to love. Yet, he'd better make sure he returned that book on time, as it was signed out on two-week loan. After all, she was still the librarian, and every single book mattered.

* * * * * * *

"I found it. Well actually the librarian found it, but none the less here it is," Joshua announced into the intercom when he reached Summer's house.

"I'll be down," Summer said into the crackling intercom.

Joshua collapsed into the mesh chair outside the purveyors of hot cocoa and candy dreams. The owners looked out the window shaking their heads and holding each other tightly. Together they said, "*Amore.*"

* * * * * * *

While Joshua waited, sweating and breathing hard, half collapsed on the table for added support, he was reminded of his last encounter with Summer's father.

"Have you discovered the ultimate truth yet, young Joshua?" Mr. Rains sat at his desk, strangely devoid of all things, tapping his precision pen on it with that look in his eyes of already knowing the answer to the question lingering so heavy in the air.

"I honestly didn't know there was one single ultimate truth, sir." Joshua was trying his best to buy a little time to think at a deeper level concerning the question that had become his overwhelming focus of attention.

"Take a moment, as you can see I've cleared both my desk and my schedule...'

Minutes of silence ensued. The quiet didn't seem to bother Mr. Rains in the least; he simply kept tapping his pen to a rhythm that was perfectly on beat, yet unidentifiable.

"Well, since GOD deals in absolute truth and not in our facts or our limited attempts at knowledge, it must be that GOD is the ultimate arbiter of truth." Joshua was very pleased with his answer.

"Please elaborate." Mr. Rains showed no reaction to the answer he was given.

"GOD knows all things, not just the physical and historical, but even more importantly, the spiritual and longings of the heart."

"And..." Mr. Rains prodded Joshua for more.

"GOD knows not only our goals and desires, but HE also knows the true motivations behind those same longings." Joshua took a deep breath, he wasn't sure he had more to offer on the deepest subject he'd ever been drawn into.

"So you're saying GOD knows all?" Mr. Rains raised a wary eyebrow, then he added the bombshell of a 'twist' to the question at hand. "What GOD are we talking about? Who's GOD?"

Immediately Joshua defended his position, "Well the only GOD! The GOD of the Bible! HE is the only LIVING GOD! All of the others are merely wood and stone devoid of power. They are shattered dreams, vacant inventions of carnal man."

Mr. Rains smiled a fatherly smile of complete respect, "Joshua, well done! You are God's faithful servant!" He laughed a knowing laugh to lighten the atmosphere that had grown so heavy. "Joshua, to answer my own question, and to condense your very adequate response, God is Truth, and as His loving Son so elegantly proved over two millennia ago, *'The Truth will set you free.'*"

Once again time froze in the Rains Estate as both Joshua and his mentor absorbed the nuances of the conversation. Only the tapping of the pen and the ticking of the clock on the shelf above made sounds to a steady beat..

"Joshua, you have permission to pursue our daughter, that is, of course, if she'll have you," Mr. Rains stated matter-of-factly with a knowing smile.

"Thank you, sir! I shall pursue with all of my heart!" Joshua didn't even know he'd answered. He felt ecstatic.

*   *   *   *   *   *   *

Fresh pulses of adrenaline shot through Joshua as the carnivorous squadron of hungry uluas burst into the inner sanctum of the lagoon once again. Splitting into two delta formations they hit the unsuspecting school of baitfish. A virtual massacre occurred as fins and tails and pieces of heads gently spiraled towards the sand and gravel floor of the ocean below. Immediately eels appeared to tear at the fragments starting to litter the seabed, including monsters and moray eels over six-feet in length with huge heads full of needle-sharp teeth. Nothing wrestled with them as they dined on the remnants by thrashing and rolling amongst the coral heads. Puffs of powder-fine sand suspended as white dust clouds in the pristine waters from their onslaughts.

The attack of the uluas were ferocious, the aftermath was primordial...

In that instant of newly released adrenaline, Joshua had a brilliant thought, he correlated the scene of the octopus skittering away towards a ravine that was opposite of where he'd been patiently waiting for his dive partner to reappear. Taking a chance, and memorizing the exact area he was hovering over, he set out to follow that ravine around the corner. As he methodically kicked that direction he prayed for a favorable outcome. It was the first time he'd prayed during this entire ordeal of being separated and lost in this unfamiliar ocean wilderness. He should have remembered earlier what Mrs. Rains had taught him in the kitchen under the auspices of helping her cook. "Joshua, it is important to pray first – then act. It's why we pray before we eat, because sometimes you never know what's really going on in the kitchen!" She had offered that bit of deep-seated truth with a giggle of mischievous knowledge he dared not inquire about.

* * * * * * *

Seeing the sweat on his brow and joy in his eyes, Summer made a snap decision. "Joshua, would you be kind enough to read the *Scroll Of Love* to me, right here, on this cool spring evening?" It was a question wrapped in a challenge as they were far from being the only people enjoying the ambiance of the beautiful evening on the busiest street in the city.

Joshua, having learned how to be bold and employing the courage he'd learned from previous requests, stood on the chair and gathered his thoughts while he thumbed through the book *Fragments Of Truths* looking for the passage that contained the requested scroll.

With all of the eloquence he could muster, and in a voice he did not know he possessed, Joshua read the scroll to Summer and the crowd that slowly gathered as his performance transfigured The Chocolatier's tiny outdoor venue into a stage.

He received a standing heartfelt ovation from his unexpectedly large and rambunctious audience. The heartiest applause came from the husband and wife that owned the quaint store. Looking approvingly at their friend's daughter and the boy they'd grown to love, they retreated back into their candy shop as it filled with newfound customers.

It seemed that both love and handmade chocolates went well together.

"Your father gave me his permission to pursue you." Joshua offered as the noise and crowd faded.

"He did, did he? I didn't know that he was in charge of such things." This was the first time Joshua had seen Summer shocked.

"I didn't either. But, since I have his permission, I intend to pursue you with all haste," Joshua announced with an air of formality.

"I would expect nothing less." Summer pulled him close and put her arm through his and leaned her head on his shoulder. Her smile conveyed an expression of her heart's content.

Two cups of hot cocoa magically appeared before them; it was gratitude for the evening's entertainment. They were a gift from the owners.

* * * * * * *

Summer became amazingly less difficult to find after the reading of the *Scroll Of Love* in public by Joshua. She gave him her phone number and told him to use it.

It appeared that they were an item!

Towards the very end of the semester, with finals scheduled and imminent, Joshua once again found his way to

Mr. Rains for another round of conversation. Mr. Rains began, "It is important that you learn how to not just make a living, for any man worth his salt can do that, but how to actually create and manage wealth. It is important for not only you, but for those God will entrust into your care."

He looked at Joshua as he continued the weekly lesson. Everything he was grooming this young man for wasn't simply out of kindness, it was to pass on wisdom to the next generation and to create a dynamic for his daughter to live well should she choose to create a life with this young fellow. In a way, it was a means of self-defense for the daughter he loved.

"There are three ways of making a living. They are very simple both in concept and the reality they each obtain...

"First: You bring in less money than you spend. This method is a form of continuous ruin. And, yes, it is a choice, as are all things. This method we'll call exactly what it is – poverty. It has no redeeming characteristics and a man's self-worth and world around him will crumble and fall into oblivion.

"Second: You bring in what you spend or slightly more than that amount, if you are lucky. Most day laborers and I include both laborers and salaried in this category, in fact most of all Americans, live in this world. This reality, even though technically not called poverty, it is still a trap that confines the human spirit to a life of mediocrity, dullness of being. Just 'getting by', as they say, is corrosive to the soul. Lingering debts, minimal freedoms, always on someone else's schedule. And, when and if you have some free time, you virtually have no money to enjoy it. This method is a dull sword, and with very limited savings, a broken shield of protection in trying times. Believe me, trying times will attempt to capture you, as they do with every soul that has ever walked the earth. Just getting by leads to a quiet desperation devoid of an outlet with no means to escape. It is a different type of poverty; it is simply poverty in slow motion. We'll call this second method of living – normal. For it is the natural state of affairs for the vast majority of those around us, being normal, is an insidious trap and captures many in its tenacious grasp of slow death.

"Then we have the third option: The option rarely taken, the pathway that incorporates all aspects of the human condition and bends them to the will of the participant, instead of crushing the participant to the will of the world. Wealth, not riches or an abundance of material things, but true wealth is the key that unlocks the magnificence of this earthly existence, making it an experience that allows your spirit to soar! Embracing this third way, by applying the *Courage of Joy*, the *Light of Brilliance* and *The Wisdom of Wealth* are the keys that unlock the magnificence of this earthly adventure. All wrapped in the hope of a better tomorrow, they give you freedom. And freedom, young Joshua, gives you the inherent joys of time as you wish. As you desire. Time to laugh. Time to rest. Time to run the race set before you. Time to explore this breathtakingly beautiful planet on which we all sojourn together through both space and time. Time enough to dream. And, as we discussed, time is the most valuable commodity of all.

"This third option, the option called wealth, is when you choose to have more money than you can spend. Simply put, the funds that you generate from your activities greatly exceed your expenses. By creating that dynamic, you no longer just get by, you can truly prosper. And, by prospering, you become a blessing to all around you. Not just those you love, but even for people you will never meet. To people you will never know, for as an overflowing cup, the wealth you produce will spill over on those who desperately need it.

"Choosing wealth makes you a formidable warrior in the ongoing battle between good and evil, this war that is as old as time itself. It brings the light of CHRIST into the darkness that ensnares so many tepid souls with wicked designs.

"Wealth is not easy, obvious, or a path that is without peril or risk. In fact, it is a most dangerous journey that is fraught with more perils that you could possibly choose. Yet, that choice is more than worth all of the risks that shall occur along the way! For, true wealth is the only option that transcends all and creates a world worthy of living within. Wealth is time, freedom, joy, and love all combined with the reserves to pull others upward to a better place. Where dreams are not just possible, but can be brought into a reality of fruition.

"Wealth is not a lineal equation, but it is a three-dimensional state of being that leaps into the future and bursts upward with inspiration. It is the way that encompasses the very essence of the prosperity that GOD's only SON, JESUS describes as an attribute he desires for each and every one of HIS created beings to prosper within and possess in great abundance.

"For, young Joshua, all of us truly are HIS *Children Of Light* and HE sings our truths eternal."

* * * * * * *

Joshua slowly kicked above the coral encrusted grotto shining in a multitude of colors from the beams of light dancing and walking across its odd and strange topography. From his newfound vantage point he'd decided to follow the path that the octopus had taken around the rock wall, but not before dialing in his compass – putting the red of the needle at the gateway from where the squadron of uluas emerged out of the open ocean. He did not wish to learn what was out there, at least not on this dive.

He allowed his gauges to fall away and trail by his side. He knew time was not on his side. Not any longer. Whatever was going to transpire needed to happen in short order; there was fourteen minutes of air remaining and it was rapidly dwindling down. Having decided to try to find his wayward dive partner, his exertions would consume his reserves at a much more rapid pace.

Joshua instinctively patted the round object in his vest pocket over his heart - it gave him a touch of joy and a burst of hope. And, as he'd been instructed, hope was a powerful force. He had a plan: he was going to reappear out of the blue waters, act as if he'd found some small treasure, then he'd get down on one knee and ask for Miss Summer Rains' hand in marriage by retrieving the gold and diamond ring in his vest pocket and offering it to her.

Here, in this pristine place, dreams appeared to become reality.

But then, his plan to acquire the forever love of Summer was now being replaced with a more pressing need, his very survival!

And at this exact moment in time, he hoped to find his dive partner.

Surely he wasn't too far...

Chapter Eleven

Once again Joshua found himself in the kitchen helping to create another culinary masterpiece with Mrs. Rains.

The food was being cooked but Joshua was being grilled and he didn't even know it!

"What are we having this evening, Mrs. Rains? By the way, I love your meals, for me they are a touch of home." Joshua made casual conversation as he dutifully grated the cheeses placed before him.

"How about macaroni and cheese with glazed ham. It's a blustery day and I feel like comfort food is in order." She smiled as she dug the ingredients out of the massive double-door refrigerator stuffed to the max.

"Some ancient secret Rains recipe?" asked Joshua, grating his third specialty cheese.

"Can you keep a secret that few know and less will ever divulge?" Mrs. Rains turned and looked at him squarely in the eyes.

"Yes ma'am, I shall take your secrets to the grave."

"Well let's hope that's a ways away! This family recipe I 'discovered' from a lady giving out samples in the local market. She probably got it off the Internet. But now it is my favorite, hopefully it will become the basis for an ancient family recipe for my grandchildren, whom I have yet to meet." Mrs. Rains looked intently at Joshua, who was blushing fifteen shades of red.

Quiet pervaded all things, only the rhythmic sound of the grating of the cheese could be heard for some time.

Seeing that she had the upper hand in the kitchen banter, Mrs. Rains subtly searched for more information. "How do you like Summer's apartment on Newbury Street? She was so fortunate to find those accommodations."

"Well, Mrs. Rains, the location is great," Joshua answered, still not grasping how he was being 'milked' for information by a master. "She's close to everything she loves; shopping, dining, all of the colleges and their multitude of theatric productions. University is only a few minutes ride away on the 'T' – her place is as convenient as can be. But, I do believe her favorite joys are her downstairs neighbors – the owners of your favorite store – The Chocolatier. They are such wonderful souls. You know, they treat us both like their children." Joshua smiled, "Hot cocoa on a cold city day is awesome, and when it's occasionally free, it is even better."

"You know, they were never able to have children, I think you have been adopted." Mrs. Rains became very serious in a loving kind of way. "You should take the time to get to know them – they may be older – but their story is amazing and I am sure that they would love to share it with you."

Joshua nodded his head and moved on to the next varietal of cheese to add to the pile.

"How do you like the décor of Summers' apartment? She spent a lot of time decorating it." Mrs. Rains posed the question as she started stirring the cheese into the noodles to create her Five-Cheese and Macaroni 'future family legend' of a meal.

Joshua, not getting a mother's ways, and that this was the real answer to her deepest question of which she had been searching for. "I don't know, she has never invited me past the doorbell, Mrs. Rains."

Mrs. Rains gently laughed. She relaxed after finding out the nature of the relationship between her loving daughter and this 'certain young man.' She now liked Joshua even more. And, she trusted the judgment of her daughter more than ever. It made her spirit leap for joy, truly lighter than angels' wings!

* * * * * *

"Congratulations on graduating from Harvard, Joshua, that is quite the achievement. Also, I hear you have found gainful employment," Mr. Rains said. It was their weekly time that they spent together. Mr. Rains had to modify his schedule to an early evening hour so as to accommodate Joshua's newfound obligations.

"It's in construction, although my job has been to tear things down so they can be re-built to new specifications. Technically that would make it deconstruction, so to speak." Joshua was tired it had been a very long physical day of hard labor.

"How does it feel?" Mr. Rains asked, honestly engaged in the topic at hand.

"Good. Very good actually. After all these years of only ever reading about and discussing the human endeavor of engineering and applied physics, I now get to live it...and the pay is better than I've ever known." Joshua' s fatigue showed when he added, "Although I'm too tired to even notice since I have almost zero time to spend it." Joshua was just noticing the dichotomy of the situation he now found himself within.

"So many deep truths in your single statement. But yet, the base truth, the heart of the matter if you will, is that work is your friend." Mr. Rains cut through everything to get to the base rock of the subject at hand.

"I certainly sleep better," Joshua commented as he rested fully relaxed in the overstuffed chair in the corner of the den.

"Alright, let's sum this up, shall we? Work equals income, work equals new hands-on learning experiences and work equals a well-earned deep night's sleep." Mr. Rains raised an eyebrow, as he often did when he was searching for more as he leaned in towards his young protégé. "Anything else you might be learning?"

"Hard work is a new environment for me, and now that I am immersed within it, I strangely like it. I honestly look forward to waking up early and getting back at it. I can see progress every day – unlike academia, the world I come from – there is great satisfaction in setting myself to a task and seeing a job well done." Joshua smiled, mostly to himself as he went on with his observations. "Work gives me a sense of value that I have never known until this point in time."

Mr. Rains beamed while hammering his point home. "I am proud of you Joshua, as I said before: *work is your friend.*"

* * * * * * *

Joshua swam at a brisk pace. His simple plan was to complete a large figure eight to maximize his coverage without losing the one advantage he had, which was a sense of the perceived safety of staying within the confines of Heaven's Threshold. If he left the main area of this dive site, he was afraid he would never make it home.

Suddenly, off to the edge of his vision, he saw a group of predator-hunters come around the corner of an up-thrust reef section. Together they started working the reef below him. Like a hungry pack of baby wolves, working methodically together as one well trained unit, a school of black tip reef sharks started stealing the remnants of the ulua's attack that littered the oceans' floor. Without regard for the needs of any of the other bottom dwellers they took any and all that they could find. Eventually they came into a direct confrontation with one of the huge moray eels that unexpectedly found itself cornered against the base of a lava pinnacle. Without remorse or hesitation two of the small 2-3 foot long black tip sharks flew into the eel with wild abandon. A tremendous fight ensued. Rolling and battering the sharks with its 6 foot long body of nothing but muscle, it appeared that the eel had a fighting chance. However, that was until another black tip joined the fray – making it three on one. When it clamped its serrated jaws into the base of the eel's head, nearly decapitating it in the process, the battle was won. Immediately more sharks joined in to complete the dismembering of the eel as it was torn to shreds and consumed.

Joshua had never seen anything like it! He was mesmerized by the carnage that exploded into a feeding frenzy just below him. He fell into absolute survival mode as his adrenaline kicked into high gear; he had the startling revelation that it could have been him!

Trying his best to be invisible and distance himself from the war zone, he knew without a shadow of a doubt it was time to find his dive partner and get back to the safety of land. After what he'd just witnessed, anything above the water would do. He was in a foreign space that had just confirmed his deepest suspicions; he was not only out of his element, but, in this liquid world, he wasn't at the top of the food chain either.

* * * * * * *

"Are you brave enough to love fearlessly?" Mr. Rains asked on a windy day, as he and Joshua waited for the evening's meal to be served.

"I hope so," Joshua answered. He was tired as could be after another crazy day of intense physical labor.

"Not just those around you, but even yourself?" Mr. Rains asked the second part of his lingering question.

"I'm not sure what you mean, sir." Joshua perked up and realized that the questions had real merit and he didn't have anywhere near a real answer to give.

"Then, young man, I believe we've found your next assignment." Mr. Rains got up and bid Joshua to follow. "Care to walk with me? Let's discuss the different ways to value 'stuff.' This is a lesson I learned later in life than I should have."

As they walked the halls through the various rooms of the rambling home, which was even larger than it looked from the outside, and it was formidable from the outside, Mr. Rains started pointing out items of interest. "Here we go, one of my favorites, a small sculpture from Outer Mongolia – this bronze is from an unknown era by an unknown artist. Price unknown as well, but, for me, the value is immense. I simply love this piece! You see, for me, it is the epitome of action frozen in time. Yet, even more importantly, it was a gift that taught me a lifelong lesson that I sorely needed to learn just then."

"What was that lesson, if I may?" asked Joshua as he inspected the intricate figurine of a Mongolian warrior riding like the wind on a horse gone mad.

"That there is unwarranted kindness in this fallen world - an absolute true kindness – even from total strangers." Mr. Rains got completely lost in the moment.

Continuing on they stopped at a painting displayed majestically by itself above an ornate table. "See this painting? It is by an artist who never made a penny on it. But yet, I paid an outrageous amount of money for it at an auction house in Hong Kong." Mr. Rains let that sink in, then he added the real wisdom he wished to impart. "Unrewarded genius is so common that it is barely even worth mentioning."

That truth rattled Joshua, and he couldn't help but reply, "You mean everyone made money on this artist's efforts except for him – the one that took the time, the extraordinary effort to create such an obvious masterpiece?"

"It happens so often that the term 'everyday' isn't accurate enough, it should be every second of every day." Mr. Rains clarified his statement as he too shook his head in disbelief.

Joshua stopped and admired a small box made from a wood he couldn't identify, but as he gazed at the grain patterns they danced as holograms giving it a three-dimensional illusion of movement. "What is this made from?" Joshua was enthralled by the patterns as he picked it up to inspect its beauty even closer.

"That is koa, found only in Hawaii. It's probably the most desirable, and expensive, wood on earth. It is rare, beautiful with delicate grain that explodes with vibrant motions of color. I've always thought that man takes too much credit for inventing holograms and 3D, once you've seen koa up close you know that GOD was way ahead of us in those arenas of visual experiences – as HE is in every aspect."

"Where did you find that box? On one of your many travels?"

"From my workshop, at times a man needs a hobby." Mr. Rains laughed out loud, "Especially with three women in the house!"

They both laughed until it hurt. As the tour continued towards the kitchen, which called their names with smells of supper gently wafting down the corridors of masterpieces and mementos, both that had valuations based on the heart and not man's price tags.

Quickly the tour came to an abrupt end, as delicacies called to them with promised seats at a bountiful table. This overcame mere possessions, since home cooking trumped all things.

* * * * * * *

After dinner, or supper as they so quaintly called it, Mr. Rains continued the tour...

Joshua went first, "So I'm noticing a trend, you intersperse hand-crafted items; some by you, the girls, your wife, along with other artists that are completely unknown with museum quality works of immense value. I find that strange, but in this setting, they blend exceedingly well."

"Two separate valuations. I'm not showing you all of these 'things' to brag, I'm giving you this tour for two purposes. First is for you to realize that my valuations are different than what and how the world places values on objects. These handmade items; the oil paintings by Summer, the quilts by my talented wife, the figurines by our baby girl, even my boxes all have a much greater value to me. They will always be dearer to my heart than the Mattisses, the Rubens, the Rembrandts and all of the other masters' works. You see, and I quote, 'value is in the eye of the beholder.'"

"What is the second point? For I easily understand the first point that you are making, which is as old as time."

"That these are all just things and have zero inherent value of any kind. Stuff is stuff." Mr. Rains got very pointed and wanted this wisdom to not be missed, so he took his time to look directly at Joshua as he continued. "These items, irrespective of whether they are worth a few dollars or millions of dollars, are all just stuff. Pretty wood glued together. Paint carefully applied to canvas. Clay formed, glazed and fired to appear to be something it is not. All just stuff, no matter their cost or perception of value, these items cannot buy one minute of time, a smile from a loved one, a dance of joy, a single moment of happiness. Stuff has no value when times of war pursue you, when famine destroys the land."

Mr. Rains went on, as tremendous feelings penetrated his speech, "Stuff will be the last thing on your mind when peril invades your world and your next breath may be your last."

With a deep sigh of profound truth, he gazed at Joshua, "Stuff you can possess, but you must be ever vigilant that you never allow stuff to possess you."

Joshua nodded as they continued on their journey, a journey that had almost nothing to do with man's riches or mankind's failed truths.

Chapter Twelve

He had to find his dive partner – it was critical. Joshua grasped the concept, after evaluating the facts at hand. The pack of sharks, his dwindling air supply, and being completely lost was a recipe for disaster. It was time to go. Flee might be a more appropriate word.

Then, halfway through his figure eight recon mission, Joshua spotted what he'd so desperately needed to see and hope began to soar within him.

A column of bubbles rose above a small wall of coral encrusted lava a few ravines over – those bubbles of compressed gases rapidly expanded as they climbed to join with the violent whitewater pressing down.

He'd found his dive partner! He headed in that direction without hesitation – all the while the scene of the giant moray eel getting torn to shreds played in his mind as an endless loop. He might be able to deal with one or two of the baby sharks, but when the third and fourth joined in he would become a goner, shredded and eaten without remorse.

The thought of it made his skin crawl, so he put it aside, braved up and swam for the safety of his newly rediscovered dive partner and eventually the way home. It was none too soon, as he glanced at his gauges on his way to find his dive partner.

Joshua had nine minutes of air and a heart beating like war drums to battle...

* * * * * * *

"How about one more assignment? It has been awhile since you dared me to learn something of value," Joshua said to

Summer on a warm late August evening. "I miss your training exercises, and a spiritual challenge would do me good, physical labor has its limitations." Joshua was completely exhausted from the months of hard labor, which had no end in sight.

Summer needed not to think too long; after all she'd been plotting this very thing for a while. "How about you create something of real value for me and yourself?" She hugged him as they walked in the cool of the shade along Newbury Street as the sun evaporated the day.

"Like what exactly? I do demolition which doesn't lend itself to works of art." Joshua laughed at the irony of the moment and the request at hand.

"You've read the scrolls: *Courage, Wisdom, Light, Love* and *Joy*. How about you write one for me? For yourself. For prosperities sake!" Summer stopped and looked up at him with her eyes of blue that transcended time and space. "Write a scroll called *Hope* - you can do it – I know you can!" Then she giggled, "Write it in English if that helps!"

Laughing along with her light hearted joke, Joshua nodded his approval and continued to walk his girl home.

That's right.

His girl!

Down the street of chocolates and dreams...

* * * * * * *

Finding his dive buddy wasn't exactly turning out the way he'd hoped, something was desperately wrong. He found him wedged into a small half-moon opening at the base of a lava wall that went all the way up into the foaming chaos high above. His legs and fins would thrash about wildly as a mix of sand and debris created a rolling cloud of off-white in the crystal clear waters. Then they would stop, pause, then thrash wildly again.

As Joshua swam down and around the outcropping to get a closer view, he saw that his partner was trapped by an odd circumstance in a very tight spot. Every time he tried to back out of the mini-cavern, his dive gear would twist allowing his tank to turn at a ninety-degree angle. That twist of his tank and buoyancy compensator would force his buddy down and into the hard-packed sandy bottom.

How long he'd been trapped here was unknown, however, where he was would be nothing but easy pickings for the pack of hunter-killers that couldn't be too far behind them.

What Joshua couldn't see was that every time his dive partner tried to extricate himself, his hose would kink and cut off his air supply. Consequently, what had been an annoyance had now become life threatening and his scuba diving partner was quickly approaching sheer panic.

Joshua wasn't bound by any of the previous efforts or feelings of doom, so he swam down, wedged one of his fins against a section of coral on the lava wall and the other fin on a rock outcropping in the sand. Then he grabbed his dive partner by the ankles and pulled hard with all of his might...

* * * * * * *

"Let's talk about applied leverage, surely in your demolitions you have learned about various usages of applied leverage?" Mr. Rains, always the master teacher, half asked half informed Joshua of the topic at hand.

"Every day I use leverage; crowbars, hammers, and ripping bars," Joshua answered, not at all sure where this topic was headed.

"Then you understand the concept as it pertains to physics. But, do you understand the concept as it pertains to business? That by taking even tiny amounts of capital you can control large amounts of property, and in the process, create opportunities that most people are unaware of?" Mr. Rains looked intently at Joshua as he spoke. "Leverage is the key when you are starting out. It is more than essential. It is absolutely critical to obtaining a large portfolio of assets in a short period of time. It is how you become a man of substance. It is how you obtain assets like real estate, especially in the sector of natural resources; timber, natural gas and oil reserves, as well as mineral rights such as aggregates and ores. It also applies to assets like stocks, bonds, precious metals and even cash reserves – in every case leverage is a key that will unlock the mechanism of being able to transfer true wealth to whomever pursues it.

"Much like applied physics and building construction, or in your case deconstruction, leverage applied correctly is everything and creates the outcome you desire to happen."

Mr. Rains looked at Joshua, leaned forward and continued. "Save up one month's pay from your hard work and efforts, we'll meet again and see what and where that small beginning takes us." Mr. Rains stood and turned, holding his arms wide. "Maybe that journey will lead you to a place like this loving home we enjoy so much."

On the way back into the city, Joshua pondered the implications. He honestly didn't know what to make of it all, but he certainly hoped so!

*   *   *   *   *   *   *

Joshua stood, feeling more nervous than ever, before the toughest audience he could ever imagine. It was amazing that a small gathering of four souls could make him quiver in his socks: Summer, Mr. and Mrs. Rains, and the ever-effervescent little sister, who he'd finally learned was called April. They all sat in the living room of the Rains Estate smiling and waiting for Joshua to read his latest assignment with great flair and theatrical eloquence, as Summer had instructed.

"Wait, one more thing." Mr. Rains held up his hand just as Joshua was about to begin. "I do believe we need a dramatic backdrop." Mr. Rains pushed a button on a small remote and a deep sapphire blue fire erupted in the fireplace. Perfectly on cue, as to accentuate the 'stage.'

"That's cheating," Joshua blurted out. He'd never seen anything like it, a fireplace with a push button remote control.

"Cheating is for tests in school, fraud, and thefts. It is the opposite of applied honesty and any effort of righteously earned wages or grades." Mr. Rains held his position, "In the real world this is called efficiency." He chuckled, allowing the atmosphere to settle. "Please, young sir, at your leisure..."

Joshua unfurled his handmade scroll, and with great flair and imagining himself victorious after slaying an ancient dragon, he read his piece of literature. He hoped his attempt at inking a tiny bit of immortality was worthy of his audience.

Upon completion, the crowd sat in stunned silence. They then slowly stood and went wild with applause! Well, for them it was the equivalent, as they all stood, smiled, and gave a hearty golf clap. Young Miss April even gave him a hug of intense joy. Then, as was usual, she skittered to points unknown by sliding down the hallways and turning the first corner while drifting in her socks without a sound.

Joshua felt like he'd slain his phantom dragon and all was well. This was acknowledged by the warm smiles of honest joy emanating from his newfound family.

"Might that original scroll be for us?" Mrs. Rains asked with a loving smile.

"Of course! I was hoping you would accept this as a gift for all of the meals you've created and for all of your kindnesses that rescued me when I needed them most." He offered the scroll with a sweeping bow and outreached hands.

* * * * * * *

One week later, on his way back to Mr. Rains' den for his weekly tutoring on the wisdom of wealth, he noticed that a painting had been removed, a masterwork by the great American painter, Andrew Wyeth, if he remembered correctly. And there – prominently displayed for all to see – was his *Scroll Of Hope*.

His scroll was not a masterpiece by the world's standards, but it obviously held great value to those who really mattered in his world.

It made his heart leap for joy and soar like an eagle on a warm summer's day!

* * * * * * *

With concentrated effort and perfectly applied leverage, Zachariah Nalu Rains, Summer's distant cousin, son of the Governor of Hawaii, was extricated out of the half-moon mini-cavern by Joshua's very first attempt of applied leverage.

It was a miracle! Joshua immediately felt that prayer works, even in the deepest waters.

Hallelujah!

Zachariah was completely disoriented. Yet, being the waterman that he was, he took off his mask, dumped the sand that annoyed him back onto the ocean's floor where it belonged, put his mask back on and cleared it by blowing compressed air from his nose and resetting it properly on his face. He could see again! And he was free! Surveying his scrapes, bruises, and reef-cuts with blood seeping from a multitude of small slices and punctures – he reeled in his dive gear. Reattaching his gear, only his death-grip on his mouthpiece had kept everything together, he experienced a moment of pure joy. When he reset the emergency release mechanism, he realized that it must have been unlatched by the jagged lava; that event is what had set his perilous entrapment into motion – it was the root cause of his near death experience.

Then, without a second of thought, Zachariah went straight back into the mini-cavern!

Joshua could not believe what he was seeing. Are all of these local boys insane? Every single time they went into the ocean they were completely fearless – as if the law of hydrodynamics didn't apply to them! Unbelievable!

Seconds later Zachariah returned with his retrieved weapon, which he had used to catch a huge flaming-red kumu. After almost dying, it was obvious that dinner was still the most important thing!

Joshua held up his gauges, grabbed Zachariah's at the same time, and compared notes by showing them to his long lost dive partner. At this depth, Joshua had seven minutes of air, and if his math was correct, as it always was, Zachariah who couldn't see his own gauges until this very moment, had less than three minutes...

Zachariah's eyes lit up real big. Without hesitation, he headed for the exit as fast as he could swim...trailing blood from the speared kumu and various parts of his own body...an exit only Zachariah knew.

Judging from the exit's extremely well hidden nature it was obvious that Joshua would have never found it.

* * * * * * *

"Have you completed your assignment concerning leverage?" Mr. Rains asked his young protégé.

"Well, if I remember correctly, you asked for me to find what the 'cool kids' are using or doing in their spare time. Then, additionally, find three manufacturers of that specific item or past time." Joshua set his exhausted body into a Corinthian leather chair to rest after his hardest days' work yet. With this paycheck and maximum overtime, he'd been able to achieve the second portion of the lesson. He now had a month's pay in his checking account. It was the most money he'd ever saved on his own. Achieving that singular goal was quite a personal victory for him.

"And, what have you found?" asked Mr. Rains, truly intrigued about the latest in tends.

"There is too much going on out there to really pin-point a true trend that engulfs the masses of youngsters which swirl around me. Yet, one thing I have noticed, is that almost everyone's backpacks are virtually empty – it appears that textbooks have gone digital."

"Who makes that product? Is it dominated by one publishing company or many?"

"Two companies appear to have captured this emerging market."

"Are either of them publically traded?" Mr. Rains asked pointedly.

"One company is. They control the majority of the educational eBooks being published for many of the universities, sir." Joshua answered.

"Then it is time to leverage the money you have worked so hard to save. Together we'll buy options as a means to leverage as many shares as possible. Joshua, I'm with you on this gambit. Let's see how time plus leverage will effect an outcome." Mr. Rains smiled; his plan could be initiated immediately.

"Just so you know, you have uncovered many truths in this one exercise. First, pay attention to the world around you –

it will supply you with endless possibilities. Second, the stock market is massive and has the ability to absorb any individual's investment whether small or large. Also, it is beyond any one person's ability to manipulate, control, or overwhelm. Third, this is a business venture that can be done in conjunction with your day job - thus maximizing your efforts. Fourth, you can now make money, if you are diligent and frugal - even when you sleep. Fifth, you may be right or wrong on this new avenue you are pursuing, but either way, it is a calculated risk – learning how to take and manage risks is how you will learn the joy of reaping vast rewards."

Joshua sat straight up in his chair. He'd never thought this whole exercise through far enough to understand the ramifications and potential rewards involved. He was re-invigorated with energy. The thought of having a future whereby he could acquire both wealth and freedom had never crossed his mind.

That was, until this very instant, as a new hope invaded his world.

Chapter Thirteen

Joshua swam right on the heels of Zachariah as they swim-sprinted through the maze of coral ravines that interconnected and took them towards shore...

Towards safety...

Towards non-compressed air...

Towards Summer, who was waiting for him on the beach. Instinctively he patted his vest pocket, the one over his heart - nothing had changed – the small diamond ring was still there.

Suddenly Zachariah stopped his forward motion, turned with a wild look in his eyes, and motioned for Joshua to share his air – he had hit the end-of-the-line on his. Without any hesitation, Joshua took the regulator out of his mouth and handed it to him. Zachariah took three deep breaths before handing it back. Joshua promptly tore his SpareAir mini-bottle from its Velcro attachment, that his dad had given him for Christmas with the words, "You may never know when a few extra breaths will make all of the difference." Joshua gave the miniature compressed air safety device to his grateful partner. With Zachariah's air needs at least temporarily under control, they had but one thing on their minds, and once again, they navigated the ever-shallower waters to try and obtain a safe exit...

To Summer...

To air in abundance...

All Joshua could hear was the mechanical breathing of his regulator...

Air in...

Click.

Air out...

Click.

Air in...

Click.

Air out...

It was like the ticking of an internal clock that portrays time as an endless procession of perfectly punctuated moments without any relenting.

But, when time is air and two desperate souls are using the last vestiges of scuba tanks both large and small, neither one with any type of reserve, time becomes finite and is no longer on your side.

* * * * * * *

"Let's talk about planning and diligence," Mr. Rains offered to Joshua as the topic at hand.

"I will do my best, sir." Joshua responded with a quiet smile.

"Keep your planning simple, no more than three steps if possible. Basically: evaluate, negotiate, acquire when you are buying. Or, if selling: market, negotiate, sell." Mr. Rains saw that Joshua sort of got it, but maybe needed a more dramatic presentation.

"You see, Joshua, if you try to over think these two processes – both buying and selling – you will lose your momentum. You will lose your ability to compete and actually complete transactions. Too much time spent on evaluations or studies, too many efforts on background noise and distractions will destroy your chances. Keep it simple – believe me three steps done properly and executed quickly will always create better results than a multitude of plans, dodges, and maneuvers. This is true every single time, without exception."

Mr. Rains stood, stretched and walked over to lean on the corner of his desk. Then he continued, "Complexity only benefits the party in power. The more complex the transaction, the better it is for the person or entity holding the strings of power and control. Politics is an absolute prime example of such and it is a trait of mankind's folly. Those in control embrace complex systems. For it is within those myriads of rules, laws, regulations, fees, fines, and endless bureaucratic red tape that they can control everything and everybody." Mr. Rains changed back to the subject at hand with a deep sigh. "But in business and in your quest for wealth acquisition, you do not have the luxury of time or the resources to play such foolish games. So simply put, don't do it.

"Keep it simple; evaluate, execute, complete. One. Two. Three and done." Mr. Rains smiled. He always liked it when he could clarify a point down to its essence.

Joshua, in deep thought allowed the long pause to linger in the air...

"You mentioned two items, sir. That was about planning, what about diligence?"

"Diligence is simply consistency of thought and memory. Consistency is having clear memories of prior events, and not having to learn the same things over and over again. You will make mistakes because it is human nature to do so. We all make mistakes – and believe it or not – not all mistakes are bad. Some work out perfectly, joyfully, lovingly wonderful! Some mistakes will be the best things that will ever happen to you. In fact, it is from a mistake that I am here and married to my loving wife, Grace. You see if I hadn't been early to class on a beautiful summer's morning I wouldn't have met her. I misread the class schedule and showed up way early – yet by that mistake I gained her love, a family, two wonderful daughters and a quest to do better and make a life built around them." Mr. Rains had to stop and regroup his emotions. Then, after the needed pause he went deeper, "Sometimes mistakes are a gift from a loving GOD."

Joshua nodded, although he still hadn't understood the real gist of the point so he raised an eyebrow. Of course Mr. Rains understood the visual cue and reverted to the lesson at hand.

"Most mistakes are just that, mistakes of either poor planning or inattention to detail. Poor planning is a choice and should rarely be the cause. Yet, inattention to detail is something you must guard against and be vigilant to never ignore. You must learn to be ever attentive to the nuances of a conversation, micro-expressions and stray comments. Notice the little things and the big things will not escape you.

"Diligence is applied attention and being precise in how you use those gleaned factual bits of knowledge. In fact, diligence is much like truth, it is a long string of divergent facts correlated to the event, then taking action that transcends the facts given with the gleaned truths at hand." Mr. Rains smiled at his summation.

"So you are saying: Keep planning simple and diligence uses truth within that plan?" Joshua perked up as he simplified the entire hour's conversation into a single sentence.

"Yes!" Mr. Rains nodded vigorously. "Perfect! You have it Joshua, you get an A+ on this one!"

Young Miss April Rains burst into the panel covered room with the maps and artifacts of great value, ignored it all, and in her glorious singsong voice announced with great flair,

"Supper is ready! Hurry! I'm starved!" She immediately spun back around and went sprinting, sliding and drifting back the polished floors towards the aromas of glorious smells which wafted down the hallways creating a warmth of a welcoming home.

The estate that was filled with love, kindness, and joy unbounded; it was built with both planning and diligence. And, as is the true state of mankind's walk upon the earth, a bit of chaos and mistakes that were often turned into righteous wonder by a loving and benevolent GOD ALMIGHTY who saw all things and enjoyed blessing even the 'mistakes' of HIS children.

* * * * * * *

Noise from the dive regulator was all Joshua could hear as Zachariah pulled him up and into the chaos of the foaming mass of the whitewater overhead...

It was a mechanical sound of the regulator performing as designed...

On inhale...

Click.

Off exhale...

Click.

On inhale...

Click.

Off exhale...

Click.

On inhale...

It was if the very hand of GOD hit them as they thrust upward into the rolling walls of liquid thunder, maddened with fury. Joshua didn't know if this was truly the way out or not, but he'd been dragged here by his only hope of survival, and at this stage he was fully committed. Turmoil engulfed him as he found himself getting rolled on a rock ledge, tumbling as he tried to protect his head as he bounced off the sharp lava rock bottom with impact after horrendous impact.

In the turmoil and chaos, Zachariah lost his grip on Joshua as they were torn apart from each other.

Then, all of a sudden, it stopped. He saw a brilliant light pressing down with a silhouette standing over him; it was Zachariah with the sun high above. Immediately two hands grabbed him by the vest and lifted him to his feet. Zachariah was starring him right in the face; he spun around to see the next huge wave bearing down upon them. That is exactly when he heard but one word, shouted directly into his ear with tremendous force: "Jump!"

With that command, Joshua jumped while Zachariah lifted him upward so as not to be pummeled on the liquid cheese grater they were standing upon. One huge wave engulfed both of them sweeping them across the jagged shelf in a white foaming tempest while tremendous forces pressed in on every side.

Yet, somehow, the sound of the regulator, which Joshua clenched with a death grip between his teeth, maintained a steady rhythm.

On inhale...

Click.

Off exhale...

Click.

Chapter Fourteen

"How is our stock doing? The one concerning the eBook version offerings of college textbooks?" Mr. Rains asked, hoping Joshua had been diligently tracking it.

"It is up over twenty-two percent since we purchased it one month ago." Joshua smiled.

"If we sell now, how would that effect your month of pay that you invested?"

"Well, by exercising the options purchased and the leverage they provided, I will have accrued a little over three months' pay in profits, sir."

"Excellent! Time to sell. No one ever goes broke by making a profit. And, this favorable turn of fortune brings us to today's topic of discussion." Mr. Rains smiled, very pleased with the outcome for his young apprentice. He loved this particular subject – for this was the exact time to teach his fellow traveler the key to obtaining true wealth that transcends the world's ability to keep a person from freedom while embracing the over-flowing kindnesses that GOD designed HIS children to enjoy.

"Let's talk about *Cycles*." Mr. Rains set his reading glasses aside and handed a small calculator across the desk to Joshua. "OK, young man, please use that calculator in your hands to do the following series of multiplications. This is easy math that reaches astronomical numbers rather quickly."

Mr. Rains leaned back in his well-worn leather chair, put his hands behind his head, and relaxed as he started his dissertation about *Cycles* and the implications of the task at hand. "Our basic premise for this exercise is to race past the world's demands: taxes, fees, obligations of rent, food, clothing, utilities, fuel and basic transportation and other such necessary items. All of these, and many more, wish to steal the wealth you create; wealth of wages paid or money earned in transactions, just like the money you have created by your wise investment in choosing the correct stock. Everything that is all around us, the world we are suspended within, constantly – both day and night – tries to take our money. It literally demands it, for taxes shall be taken at a point of a gun. Make a little and they take it all. Make more and they take almost all of it. The only solution to this created barrier is to race past it without remorse! You see, young Joshua, the world perceives money differently than you or I. For them - the politicians, tax collectors, despots and mega-corporations – money is power. Right now, at this point in time, they have the reigns to that hold on power and they grasp it with an iron fist if need be. At least their perception of power – and they are not about to let go...

"Not now...

"Not into the foreseeable future..."

Mr. Rains sighed, as this portion of his dissertation gave him deep uneasiness. "With vast sums of money they can control the flow of enterprise and therefore the flow of nations. If this were accomplished in a righteous way and for legitimately wholesome reasons, I would not have such trepidation about their schemes and methods. But we live in a fallen world run by people and states that have wicked agendas...

"Today, you will learn the secret to obtaining real wealth. How to race past these manmade barriers, fortresses of design to keep you in your place as a subject of their earthly kingdom and not allow you to take your rightful place as an heir to the KING, and HIS Kingdom of Heaven. Initially you will see this as a battle of the world around you. Yet, eventually you will see it as the spiritual battle that it is. A war that wishes to destroy your essence by taking your means to transcend this earthly platform and reach a new vantage point that allows you to achieve great things, both in this world and in the heavens above."

Mr. Rains became extraordinarily animated; he held his arms high for dramatic effect and made his point abundantly clear. "You must make money, gain assets, and acquire true wealth tremendously faster than the world can strip it away from you."

Relaxing a bit, he continued. "You have to learn how to transcend the demands of your obligations, which are necessary and endless, by creating wealth in such abundance that you become a free man devoid of the world's demands upon you and your precious time."

"How do I do that? The task seems so overwhelming. Sir, I do not come from a wealthy background. Right now I have three months' pay and a half-a-tank of gas in a car with almost two hundred thousand miles on it! My Honda burns a quart of oil every other tank of gas! Joshua blurted out, concerned about his abilities to put into motion any such grand design.

"First of all, put your fears aside. After all, you understand courage, so combine that lesson with the fact that you are worthy. GOD ALMIGHTY put you here, at this exact time, in this exact place. HE knows you by name! So brave up and learn the basics of wealth creation by employing simple math and knowing how to break the system that the world puts in front of you. Employ the system that GOD blesses you with." Mr. Rains calmly delivered the answer to Joshua's deep-seated fears.

"Let's talk about *Cycles*. Not moon phases or months on a calendar, nor tides or seasons. *Cycles* as it pertains to crashing headlong through the walls erected before you and having the blessing of becoming an over-flowing cup to all around you. Are you ready?" It really wasn't a question, just a means to get to the heart of the topic at hand.

"Yes, I think so."

"The parameter of the equation is as follows: Every time you double your net worth it is equal to one *Cycle*. Starting with one dollar and using the shortest month of the year, February, if you were to double your money every day for the entire month, how much would you have at the end of that month? It is the shortest month of the year – exactly four weeks in duration." Mr. Rains looked at Joshua and nodded for him to begin as he handed him a notepad to write down the answers as he went. "Take one and multiply it by two, then keep multiplying the answer by two. Please do it twenty-eight times in total. Remember each time you multiply by two equals one *Cycle*, please call them out as you write them down."

Joshua did as instructed. "One. Two. Four. Eight. Sixteen. Thirty-two..."

When he got to the twelfth day, the *12th Cycle*, he was at *$2,048.00*. Mr. Rains stopped him there by saying, "Stop! Take a good look at that number. You surely have that amount already in your hands and substantially more. Take the time to correlate the information before you, young man. You are already well beyond one third of the exercise at hand. You are on your way to your newfound goal of reaching your *28th Cycle*."

Mr. Rains smiled and declared, "Joshua, you are well on your way and you didn't even know it until this exact point in time. Well done! You are now able to perform this simple quest to wealth and freedom." Mr. Rains beamed with joy, but Joshua was still confused by the implications of this so-called method of *Cycles*.

"OK, moving forward. Keep your numbers running and keep multiplying by two, remember that each time you do so, it is one more *Cycle*."

When Joshua reached the twenty-eighth calculation, the calculator ran out of digits and flashed **>>>ERROR<<<** since it couldn't display any number in excess of one hundred million.

Time stopped, once again, as the implications of the exercise destroyed all of Joshua's preconceived notions of how the world functioned and how money was turned into vast sums from even the humblest of beginnings.

Vast wealth, unfathomable to a country boy with college debts and a battered car in desperate need of repair, Joshua was transfixed at the sheet of paper with its handwritten numbers. He could not believe that there ever could be such a simple display of how to create his longing desire to be free of the world's demands on his most precious asset: time. His time, which he had very little of since he worked six days a week, hard physical labor that demanded sleep, just enough time to rejuvenate for the next day's grinds and toils.

Looking up at his mentor, he asked the most profound question he could muster: "Exactly how do I get from here to there?" He pointed at the *28th Cycle* on his notepad that he had multiplied by long hand; it was a number he could barely grasp: *$134,217,728.00*.

Only the clock made a sound, as it had so many times in the past...

"Well, let's talk about that on your next visit. But, remember that with tremendous wealth, comes tremendous responsibilities. All you see here, all that we have, is less than one percent of the monies that have flowed through my hands. These tremendous assets that GOD entrusts me with are not for me alone. Far from it! They are for those who are bound by the darkness and yearn to be free. Frontline missions are one of my favorite causes, as are outreach programs for youth that are caught in dire circumstances. You will find that there is no limit to the needs of those around you. You will find opportunities to help in every city, province, town, and village – literally around every corner – if you choose to be observant enough to care..." Mr. Rains spoke without a shred of bragging, just a deep longing in his heart to advance the Kingdom of GOD against the relentless darkness that he saw so clearly.

All as the clock continued its methodical ticking...

Then, with a fatherly heartfelt joy of the moment, Mr. Rains walked over to where his young protégé was standing and wholeheartedly embraced him. That simple kindness stunned Joshua as Mr. Rains gently added, "GOD bless you my dear boy. GOD has a plan for both you and the journey you are embarking upon. If you remember but only one thing from this time we've spent together, please remember that truth above all others."

"I'll do my best to remember!" Joshua was so excited.

As a last admonishment, Mr. Rains offered, "Don't do anything with your newfound wealth, allow it to build as rapidly as possible. That is unless you need new tires on your car. After all, some demands of the world aren't mere desires, but are critical to your survival. Good tires will save your life, and, at times those you love." Mr. Rains looked at Joshua and reminded him, not so subtly, that his daughter's wellbeing was in his hands.

Joshua received the message loud and clear, deciding bald tires might not be wise. He could take chances with his own life, but it was not his right to put those he loved knowingly into danger, especially Summer; with her as his *precious cargo*, he did not wish for disaster.

* * * * * * *

Joshua stood quivering from head to toe on a shelf of lava rock with the water flowing by at a depth not much higher than his ankles. As it foamed and boiled it dragged him back towards the maelstrom– looking hurriedly in both directions – he realized that the beach entrance he sought was merely yards away. Then, he got pulled off balance and swept, once again, into the depths of raging tumult.

As he tumbled and rolled he felt impact after impact jolt him with tremendous forces; first he lost one fin, then the other. His mask was ripped off his face with such violence that he could feel the strap snap past his ears as it broke!

With a death grip he clenched his teeth on his only lifeline, the mouthpiece of his regulator, which was his only access to air. Amazingly it remained firmly in his jaw's grasp.

Small boulders tumbled and rolled with him in the tiny crevice that flowed back into the sea...

Back to Heaven's Threshold...

Back to deep waters...

Breath in...

Click.

Breath out...

Click.

Breath in...

Click.

Breath out...

Click.

Air was all that mattered! Then, in the briefest moment of instantaneous anxiety – that lifeline ceased - everything faded to darkness as he realized he'd finally bled his tank completely dry.

NO MORE AIR!

And where was Zachariah?! Was he meeting the same fate? Or had he gained a foothold and made it to safety? He desperately hoped so.

After all, someone had to live...

Chapter Fifteen

Tranquility enveloped him on every side.

Sitting on a ledge in his torn and shredded wetsuit he overlooked the bay he'd just been in. It was magnificent!

Crystalline waters lightly rippled on the perfectly transparent bay's surface, fish in tremendous abundance swam in schools too numerous to count. Two playful pods of dolphins burst skyward at odd times and strange angles playing here and there. One lone pure white Hawaiian tern, an angel tern, wafted inches above the living waters without a care in the world.

Brilliant white light danced all around; the towering palms behind him gave off an effervescent purity of being, an innate quality of life perfected.

Joshua marveled in the moment that had no end of terminality in sight.

All things were beyond anything he'd ever seen or imagined.

"Hello Joshua. Mind if I sit with you a while?" gently asked the bronzed giant of a man standing beside him. His voice was as quickening thunder softly lessened for the comfort of Joshua's needs.

Joshua looked up to see an ancient presence of divine glowing light; he looked Polynesian with a blood-red wrap. He had bronze skin, rippling muscles, and without footwear. Joshua scooted a few feet over and offered the gentleman his seat on the lava rock shelf overlooking the bay.

"I see you've found Heaven's Threshold. How did you enjoy your dive? Was it to your liking?" He sat down to contemplate the awesome vantage point.

"Yes, it was surreal. There were fish everywhere, and even though above me there was the tremendous chaos of massive waves crashing, where I found myself it was liquid serenity. I even became friends with a family of barber pole shrimp – that is after I fed them a fish tail that landed nearby." Joshua laughed a light-hearted laugh. *"They even tried to clean my fins. I don't think they had much success though."*

His companion gave a hearty laugh and laid his staff of quilted koa down beside him. It sparkled with a double-helix grain pattern of golden-reds and browns. Dancing as a holographic display of GOD's magnificence captured within a tree's growth rings.

He never would have noticed if he hadn't spoken with Mr. Rains about the boxes he'd created out of the same wood in his workshop.

"Might I inquire who I'm sharing the day with?" Joshua asked politely, as he had been taught by his loving parents.

"I am the Archangel Gabriel, it is indeed my honor and privilege to be here with you. HE sent me to greet you here, at this place of joy and tranquility."

Joshua smiled, then offered, *"It wasn't so tranquil just minutes ago. This place was a roaring cauldron of waves gone insane."* Joshua looked perplexed. *"You mentioned 'HE', who is HE?"*

"Our LORD, CREATOR OF THE UNIVERSE, KING OF KINGS, JESUS. HE sent me to greet you and see what it is your heart desires?" Gabriel stated as fact.

Joshua nodded. The information startled him less than it should have.

"So what are my choices?" As he looked up, once again Gabriel was standing with his staff in hand; he had a mighty countenance about him.

"You may stay with me and we'll enter the gate to the Throne Room of the LIVING GOD. Or, you can return to the chaos and thunder and to those who love you very much."

Joshua thought about it, a very deep remarkably well designed thought of significance. Within those depths of emotion he realized he could say goodbye to his parents, friends and family – for he had already done that when he went to college.

But, he couldn't say goodbye to Summer. After all, he had a whole life before him and he desperately hoped that it would include her joyful presence every step of the way.

And, hope, as he'd discovered, was a powerful force! Maybe the most powerful force in the universe.

As soon as he formulated that desire, that deepest choice, he looked up at his newfound friend, Gabriel, who said in a voice of thunder that split the air, "As it is written in the Holy Bible for all to see:

Ask, and it shall be given you; seek, and ye shall find; knock, and it shall be opened unto you: For every one that asketh receiveth; and he that seeketh findeth; and to him that knocketh it shall be opened." [Matthew 7:7-8 KJV]

Immediately Joshua found himself falling back into the ocean. It was no longer tranquil, kind or forgiving – it had returned to its original state of complete liquid tempests of rolling waves and jagged reef...

And, once again, he couldn't breathe!

He found himself gagging into the regulator he couldn't get away from!

Somehow it was beyond his ability to get it out of his clenched mouth...

He couldn't even scream!

Chapter Sixteen

Joshua decided he needed to get home, so he skipped his Friday classes; he checked his oil, added a quart, and left for his home in rural Western Pennsylvania. He missed his family and his mother's pot roast. She'd assured him it would be waiting when he arrived.

That was enough motivation to hustle. So he drove ever faster as he got through Connecticut, then New York and into the far corner of Pennsylvania. Finally, he took the Interstate Highway and onto roads he knew well.

It was dusk. He could smell the joyous aromas of his mother's dinner in the recesses of his mind, as he kept accelerating on the back roads leading to home.

The sunset to the west turned the entire sky of checkered clouds into a dappled blaze of reds, pinks, and brilliant oranges – all on a deepening blue-black backdrop.

Coming over a knoll he accelerated into a straightaway that cut through a section of hardwood forest. Oaks, maples, and hemlocks reluctantly allowed pillars of light to dance on the roadway's surface. All as the day's final moments battled with the timber's towering presence.

Approaching the mid-point of the straight section of broken asphalt – a flash of brown and white appeared from nowhere – it was a huge buck with a magnificent set of antlers. He spun the wheel to avoid powdering the animal with his Honda's front end, but his tires – that he planned on re-placing and saving a few dollars each at his friend's family garage – did not achieve the grip on the broken road which he needed to steer clear of the buck frozen in the headlights...

Skidding at a horrendous speed, completely sideways, he hit the buck with the passenger door. *Thank God I don't have anyone with me,* was the last thing that raced through his mind!

* * * * * * *

"He's awake!" Joshua's mother screamed at the top of her lungs to the nurses' station not too far away. "*Help!* Our boy needs *help*." She was frantic with worry as the nurses leaped into action.

Joshua was sitting up wide-eyed as he desperately tried to dislodge the breathing tube with both of his hands gripped around it. Only tape and some plastic straps held it in place or he'd have ripped it out by now.

One of the nurses latched onto his hands as the other grabbed his shoulders as a means of forcing Joshua to stop. Looking him square in the eyes, with a no nonsense commanding voice, she said, "We'll remove it, but if we do it incorrectly it will cause massive internal damage. Do you understand, Joshua?" She had his undivided attention.

All this transpired as the breathing apparatus maintained its unstoppable rhythm...

Breath in...

Click.

Breath out...

Click.

Breath in...

Click.

Breath out...

Click.

* * * * * * *

It was the better part of a week since he'd gotten off of the ventilator and started breathing on his own.

His mother looked older than ever before. Yet, his father stood stalwart and solid as a rock. Joshua needed that strength - his days were labored and racked with pain - it was possible that his mother needed it even more.

He couldn't fathom how much time had elapsed, and it wasn't until one of his best friends from high school gave him the 'version' no one else would tell him that he understood all that had happened. He underwent two emergency surgeries to prep him for the ventilator, which was his only chance at living. Since both of his lungs had completely collapsed. Over two hundred stitches, most of them internal, he was finally moved from the Critical Care Unit to an Intensive Care Unit. He was observed round the clock, and during all that time his parents never left his side. He needed one more delicate surgery to remove the last fragments and shards of antlers from his spleen, kidneys, and liver – which went poorly. That surgery led to massive blood loss and a secondary event where he almost died.

During those last few hours prior to waking up, he must have had a terrible reaction to the anesthesia, since he slept fitfully at best. He tossed and turned, never being able to get comfortable.

His father forlornly observed, "It is as if he is trapped under the ice on a frozen pond – unable to surface."

When he lost it and hit the deer, a beautiful twelve-point buck, he completely atomized it, exploding it into pieces as its antlers shattered the door's window, inflicting all of his wounds. Eventually he spun to a stop, never hitting another thing, some were calling it divine intervention.

It was the deer's antlers that did most of the damage. They had made it through the collapsed door as shards and splinters, many lodged into his side. A few almost made it all of the way through him!

His wreck must have been spectacular. But, since he was unconscious and the deer was pulverized beyond belief, no one would ever be able to give a report.

He'd almost died on impact, he was brought unresponsive into the ER and sent via Life Flight helicopter to the Trauma Center in Pittsburgh, where the teams patched him back together magnificently, considering the state he had arrived in.

And that - as his friend told him - was more or less what happened. With that blunt rendition, Joshua allowed his friend's storyline to be the official version of his trusty Honda's demise and how he ended up in the hospital. Joshua filed it away, as it was to become part of his knowledge base of 'non-memories.'

"So how do you like it up there? How did your first two weeks at Harvard go? Freshman in an Ivy League school, dude! Its' got to be awesome!" His childhood buddy - who worked at the local coalmines as an apprentice equipment operator - asked with honest heartfelt joy for him. After all, very few in their small town ever got to go anywhere, let alone all of the way to Harvard up in Boston.

A strange look of tremendous loss clouded Joshua's eyes.

Slowly he formed the words, which came out of nowhere. "Honestly, my dear friend, I can't wait for Summer..."

* * * * * * *

Three incredibly lonely years flowed by as he gained the limited knowledge of man's misguided facts that were paraded as wisdom. Three long and lonely years he looked for the girl with the powder blue eyes...

Virtually every day he made time to go to the library. Often he would linger at the candy store on Newbury Street hoping to see the girl that haunted his dreams.

But, as time wore on, he was starting to believe that she was a myth, an apparition from a drug-induced traumatic experience, a glimmer of hope in the night that knew not when to end.

So he lingered at the base of *Candy Mountain,* sipping hot cocoa as he dreamed dreams of grandeur while studying to fulfill his promise and duty of graduating from an Ivy League school.

A dream that excited him not and felt tarnished by his glimpses of wisdom that came to him in bits and flashes – often in the darkest of night in the deepest of sleeps.

Fragments of truths - fleeting and elusive as they come...

Chapter Seventeen

Joshua was beginning to believe that everything he'd encountered while he'd been gone during his recovery from his horrendous wreck caused by the trophy buck was an ingrained bit of imagination. After three years of college – which amounted to six semesters of classes - he'd yet to find his blue-eyed girl, Summer Rains. She wasn't in the library or anywhere else for that matter.

She was not on campus, or in any of the local shops or delis. She was not at The Common or any of the open areas of the sprawling campus known as Harvard University. What had really changed his perspective, given him pause at the deepest levels, was the salient fact that when he drove to where the Rains Estate was, and he knew the exact location by heart, there was nothing but windswept bluffs overlooking the grassy covered dunes! It was a lonely place without a trace of a mansion or manicured yard. Zero. There was no house or driveway, no structures of any kind. No Mr. Rains in his den with a fatherly smile and stories that spoke of wisdom, truths, and methods. No Mrs. Rains with her charm and ability to look past facts and wrap everything into joyous love. No Miss April Rains with her giggles and half-sliding exits to points unknown.

Nothing! It all appeared to have been a construct induced by a three day drug-fueled coma...

Just to add fuel to the fire, Joshua had never been diving in his entire life! He'd never strapped dive gear onto his shoulders or breathed compressed gases. Especially not in pristine open ocean waters at a place called *Heaven's Threshold*.

Three years with no contact. Yet, he looked every day for the girl with powder blue eyes who appeared in his dreams, and who he expected to see around the very next corner.

* * * * * * *

It was a cold fall day, without even the hint or remembrance of summer, when he took one more sojourn into the endless halls of knowledge, man's knowledge, within the university's library. He walked at a reduced pace, slower than normal; since the wreck it seemed that cold harsh weather made him hurt all over. Joshua even limped a bit from the trauma of the accident. He found himself along the far wall of individual desks, one after the other, and yet forlorn in the darkness. Seeing a lone light lit above one of the antique wooden study spots, sitting under that faint beam of hope was a person. As he drew closer he realized that they were finishing a small carving into the desktop with a nail file. Absently without any real malice – almost on remote control - were somewhat primal in how they slowly twirled the metal tip to make the final point on their simple plea for help...

Joshua looked over the shoulder of the threadbare and tattered hoodie of the lonely soul who had so clearly carved: **SAVE ME...** into the worn surface. Without hesitation, prompted by the deepest need demanding he do something he'd never done before, Joshua stopped. He placed his hand on the shoulder of the desperate soul emitting an obvious cry for help and declared with great comfort. Joshua, in a soft voice of extraordinary kindness, prayed: *"Dear FATHER, we praise You for Your love and kindness. We thank You for all You do in our lives. Please forgive us as we at times forget the wonders and depths that You take to weave together the fabric of our lives as only You know how. Please, dear LORD, grant us Your wisdom devoid of man's inferior knowledge and facts gone astray. Please wrap us in Your love anew every moment of every day, for each of us needs those tender mercies. Thank you LORD, for we know that You truly are the CREATOR of all things. Amen.*

He didn't know where that prayer had come from; it just burst out of him with a heart full of unbounded desires.

Looking up at him were powder blue eyes crying tears of joy.

It was Summer and finally she'd been found!

Joshua could not believe that he'd finally found her. A stunned feeling of profound relief rippled through his entire body, soul, and spirit.

Silence ensued far and wide - all as that one single beam of light from above intensified beyond human endeavors.

Joshua found himself kneeling beside her and holding her hand as he gazed deep into her eyes. He had begun to believe that she was a myth, a faded echo of a memory from a world that didn't exist.

Summer Rains! The fine young Miss Summer Rains was squeezing his hand as her tears flowed with such abandon that they dripped off the tips of her long hair.

She could not believe that such a gorgeously handsome young man had taken the time to pray for her. To find her here, in her longing distress, at this very time as her world spun out of control and darkness and doubts crushed her very being.

Joshua held her hand as she, without hesitation, poured her souls' turmoil upon him, a total stranger. She was not wealthy. After all, she had grown up in what was not so affectionately called the "Combat Zone" of Boston, where Chinatown and the red-light districts merged to create chaos, crime, and plunder. It was filled with thefts and robberies gone-bad, but even more so, with broken spirits and shattered hopes deferred.

Her mother and father both worked for next to nothing at the Corner Church, the one with the graffiti covered walls. It attended to the endless parade of lost souls, devoid of futures and dreams. Her mother ran the nursery for abandoned children while her father counseled wayward youths that so often got caught in the crossfire.

She grew up in that wickedly strange environment, with hand-me-downs and tainted prospects. An only child, she too was a casualty of that ongoing and endless war of massive poverty rippling through time.

She poured out her heart to Joshua in the bubble known as academia, tucked deep within the most venerated university in America. She even dared to go as far as to share her hopes and dreams – as contrite as they were. Today she had hoped to obtain a job re-stacking shelves for minimum wage to possibly help with her dream of taking night classes; maybe if she excelled, she could eventually become a day student, a real student...

How she would ever pay the astronomical tuition at Harvard was a great mystery.

But, she had a dream and hope of a better tomorrow, and, as she'd always been taught by her loving parents, hope is a powerful force.

With that comment lingering on the edge of her desperate plea for help, Joshua asked, "How are your parents?" He did not wish for her to know how much he missed them. How he longed for those long talks filled with wisdom he had with her father. And the joyous bouts of laughter and love her mother so easily displayed in the kitchen.

Not to mention the food...

With Joshua's question, Summer melted and came completely distraught. Leaning on his shoulder she cried the tears of a broken soul as she eventually released the information that pierced his heart and fully immersed him within her shattered world. Between sobs of complete despair, she said, "They have gone missing. They volunteered for a mission trip to Southeast Asia to help with a small school and orphanage that the Corner Church helps to support."

Joshua became very concerned. After all, he loved her parents! Even if they were but memories from a reality that had no basis in fact, no basis in the world he was living in now. From a place in time seemingly so far away...

"Where on earth could they be?" Joshua asked, extremely afraid to hear her answer.

"They were on the lost plane, Malaysian Air Flight 370, they were on it! 'Last minute change' was what I heard as they called me while they boarded. That was the last time I ever spoke to them." Summer cried the throes of grief as if it had happened moments before. "Not a trace of any kind has ever been found..."

Joshua tried to absorb the implications of the news. It was impossible to fathom.

"It has been months and all hope is lost." Summer poured her heart out on the first soul who'd taken the time to listen - and the empathy to embrace her - even if he was a complete stranger. But, somehow, she trusted his brilliant green eyes and his heartfelt prayer.

Together they wept.

* * * * * * *

Joshua could not believe that his *angel parents* had been on the jet that had crashed and never been found. A modern day commercial jetliner unrecovered, presumed to be in the deepest abyss of the vast Indian Ocean, gone with little trace. One of the greatest mysteries of the modern era and it had engulfed Mr. and Mrs. Rains while they'd been on a mission-of-mercy to the ends of the earth.

It gave him such pause and created a strange imbalance of epic proportions within his innermost being. Joshua was beyond lost in the whole event, not only did the news stun him, but he saw how it had shattered the very essence of the girl he'd so diligently been seeking for years. More than that, he'd been searching for his entire life.

Yet, Summer was real, so he embraced this newfound land of the living. Joshua would start doing his best to help begin healing the wounds inflicted upon his *little girl lost.*

He would use the wealth he'd been accumulating by being observant and using careful planning and extreme diligence. Joshua used his savings to move Summer to a safe place away from the dilapidated flat where she'd been left broken as an orphan. With a sincere handshake, and by paying the first and last months' rent, he moved her into the studio apartment above The Chocolatier on Newbury Street. It was overwhelming for her to have such an upgrade to *Candy Mountain*, but for Joshua it was a righteous usage of a small portion of what he'd garnered from his mentor's efforts. He felt that Mr. Rains would be happy with his choice. An added benefit was that Summer found work at the shop with the elderly couple. They adopted her as their own, and a childless couple had a touch of Summer's warmth come into their world.

As winter loomed, Joshua slowly presented Summer with the lessons he'd learned, lessons sent to him from a place that didn't exist. If Joshua dwelt on that fact too long it made his head hurt.

So he simply allowed the truth of the matter outweigh the facts of the world before him.

* * * * * * *

In Harvard's extensive library there was no wall of ancient texts written in Paleo-Hebrew on sheepskins and parchments in the blackest inks and in the most elegant calligraphy. No wall of crystal sleeves holding a treasure trove of wisdom passed down through the epochs of mankind upon the earth. No special room or airtight corridors tucked away in the furthest reaches of the library.

Those facts really made Joshua struggle with his simple plan of how to bring Summer back from her shattered world. He wanted Summer to unleash the effervescent bundle of joyful genius that he knew was inside her waiting to burst free.

Waiting to embrace the land of the living, waiting for him.

* * * * * * *

Without the wall of scrolls, without the original copies of the condensed wisdom of the ages that Summer and her family had breathed into his spirit, Joshua was at a complete loss on how to bring Summer back. How was he to ever repay the multitude of gifts that her entire family had so willing bestowed upon him? Now that he had found her, now that his search had come to a conclusion, it was anything but the outcome he desired to obtain. His Summer, the girl that he loved, was distant and broken.

He hoped her spirit was not beyond repair, so he forced himself to remember as best he could, to reenact the lessons learned so he could impart them to her. He was on a mission of love and nothing would stand in his way. Then, as he searched the net, once again, on a cold winter's night after studies and before calling it the long hard day it had been. As he lay in bed in his cold drafty dorm room tucked away on the edge of campus – he stumbled upon a thread of information. Following that tiniest shred of knowledge, he discovered the most salient of facts: it appeared that the rarest book in existence had been uploaded as an eBook for purchase. One known original manuscript in the public domain on the planet, hidden in the most obscure small town library in mid-America. How it had materialized was a great mystery. Yet, somehow it had been digitized for prosperity. Hidden within the matrix of that epic series, *Rain Falling On Bells,* were all four scrolls. Even the *Scroll of Joy* was there. It had been reformatted as an introduction given to a young woman of heroic proportions by a character named Mathias, the 'Thirteenth Apostle', which gave Joshua tremendous pause. With his discovery, and more importantly, with GOD's divine timing, Joshua started the process of enlightenment for the only girl he would ever love. He had a plan of employing the same methods of how he had been so elegantly trained by Summer and her loving parents. He would use the same techniques to restore Summer, doing his inspired best to move her beyond her grief and sorrows.

So during the course of the next few days, he hand-copied the scrolls with the blackest ink onto the finest paper he could possibly find. With diligence and extreme attention to detail he created scrolls he could challenge Summer with and draw her back to him, the real Summer, as she had been gone far too long.

Joshua built a box of quilted curly koa in a friend's workshop for Summer as a gift. He made it with brass hinges and clasp; he finished it with ten coats of highly polished lacquer, allowing the small masterpiece appear to be captured within a crystal case. The holographic wood grain, which spoke of divine creation, was marvelous to the eye of the beholder.

Upon the box he placed a handwritten note folded perfectly into a golden origami crane, on one wing it simply stated: ***UNFOLD ME...***

So she did...

My Dearest Summer Rains,

I give to you these six ancient texts. They contain a portion of the truths of the universe that GOD ALMIGHTY has created for all of HIS Children of Light:

Scroll One: "The Song Of Courage" will give you the bravery that GOD hath bequeathed for all of HIS children.

Scroll Two: "The Song Of Light" will give you the LIGHT OF THE WORLD, JESUS. For courage without the Light of CHRIST is worthless.

Scroll Three: "The Song Of Wisdom" will give you spiritual discernment that is beyond value, for it is priceless in navigating the future set before you.

Scroll Four: "The Song Of Hope" will give you a spiritual release of embracing a vividly wonderful tomorrow, since hope transcends all circumstances.

"I Choose Joy!" will allow you to live in the moment with unbridled happiness, allowing you to be an infectious force of GOD's design.

Scroll Five: "The Song Of Love" encompasses all you shall ever need, for the gift of HIS love combines all things. Love is your true inheritance. It is given freely to you, from the very dawn of creation, before time even began.

Pick twelve verses from each manuscript. Pick those that speak directly to your heart. Read them three times a day; first at the crack of dawn, again at high noon, and then aloud prior to falling asleep. Do these simple tasks with each scroll for one week, with the last and final reading being in a public place - where you must read with tremendous heartfelt wild abandon – care not who listens!

May His courage, light, wisdom, hope, and joy wrap you in love as your sorrows evaporate and your spirit soars to Heaven's Threshold and to the calming presence of your Savior! Allow these ancient "fragments of truths" to unlock your wonderful life that wishes to embrace you, as you find your way home.

This, my dearest Summer, is my heartfelt prayer for you.

Love, Joshua

Scroll One

"The Song Of Courage"

GOD ALMIGHTY – CREATOR OF THE UNIVERSE – KING OF THE ANGEL ARMIES – LORD OF LORDS – IMMANUEL

Sings All Into Creation With Courage

Courage is available to all who choose to reach above their circumstances to grasp it. Courage has no age, ethnicity, gender, physical, mental, emotional or Earthly preconditions. Courage is a gift from a righteous GOD to mortal man. When darkness is on the march looking for any niche in the armor of mortal man's hedge of protection, courage must fill the gap when all other means fail.

Dust, hail, thunder, lightning, maelstrom and raging floods all shall bow to courage.

Observe the natural world around you for endless examples of the courageous acts of GOD's smallest creatures and grasp how even the tiny sparrow attacks the raven in its midst without forethought or reservation. By its actions it draws out the courage in the flock around it, allowing for the minute to overcome the attack of the strong.

Courage may be observed by the inanimate creation from time's inception. Take for example even the rocks – for they say to the raging ocean: "This far and no further for your advance stops here!"

Courage shall not be moved, neither by threat or fire, by intimidation or violence, by hate or the conjuring of the dark forces that dwell in the hearts of wicked man.

Courage prevails against all odds. Those designed by evil men or by the circumstances thrust upon mortal man by forces beyond his understanding or control.

Courage is employed by the Angels Of Light for THE KING OF THE ANGEL ARMIES in the Heavens above, in realms unseen, unknown, unfelt.

Courage is announced by the smallest child in the tiniest of acts, acts of courage against injustice by darkness of those even smaller than themselves. For even that one small child knows to stand, fist clenched, as the forces of darkness wish harm upon their lesser brethren.

Courage dances in the face of danger and laughs at anything or anyone that even implies that GOD's wondrous joy may not be brought forth.

Courage praises the LORD as chaos descends and violence erupts upon all sides.

Courage is the gift of the divine to the weakest of souls and shall magnify those who choose to employ it.

May the Heavens fall and man be erased from the Earth if courage ever falters.

Courage never fails and the courageous shall forever and ever be victorious as mankind and all of creation races into the fires of time stretched before their infinite existence.

Courage is a valiant gift from a loving GOD.

Courage echoes from the mountains above
For the mountains sing of courageous love
May the sky quake and all of the Heavens fall
If courage cannot conquer evil's dark and lusty call

Courageous man's efforts upon this frail Earth
Will test the length, the breadth, the girth
Of darkness and pain and death's final throes
Even with those failed truths, courage still grows

No valiant man or mighty in heart
Shall ever be far from what courage can part
Frail and the simple, the small and obscure
Even those who are tiny can courage ensure

Courage dances in the face of wicked designs
Sings praises of glory with joy intertwined
May the gift of GOD's courage meet all of your needs
As bells sing in Heaven of HIS mighty deeds

Shall the gates of hell be broken
With one courageous act
Heaven's gates will be opened
For those who embrace GOD ALMIGHTY's pact

For HE swears to give liberally

To each and every soul

To those who race valiant

To the courageous bell's toll

Sing of courage!

Scroll Two

"The Song Of Light"

GOD ALMIGHTY – CREATOR OF THE UNIVERSE – KING OF THE ANGEL ARMIES – LORD OF LORDS – IMMANUEL

Sings All Into Creation With Light

When all was darkness, void, decrepit, absent of all life – GOD THE CREATOR spoke and a tremendous light shown forth. Light that illuminated HIS very presence, announced to the vast and furthest reaches of darkness: here I AM and MY light shall forever more shine forth.

Here I AM and there is no other.

Light was the creation that overwhelmed all with its glory.

Within that light were all of the attributes of the GOD OF CREATION: Love, kindness, courage, wisdom, acceptance, truth, joy, hope and grace. Boldness and mercy along with all that is good, pure, and holy are aspects of this same light – the spark that set all things ever created into motion.

Everything ever created and of creation, the Earth, the moon, the sun, the stars, all of the orbs of light of the night and that which blazes in the daytime. All that there ever was, is, and will be springs forth from that light.

Light allows even the tepid souls to see their way; it allows one to see another, their hopes, dreams, passions, along with their needs, wants, desires.

Light within the eyes of man cannot be hidden from those whom choose to see.

Light conveys hope of a joyful dawn to a world that so desperately needs that very message daily from their CREATOR to HIS created mortal men upon the Earth below.

Light wavers in the wind, dances upon the waters, and walks upon the mountaintops for all to see, for all to take notice, for all to witness the glory of creation through all of the eons of time.

Light filters through the tiniest of cracks to illuminate that which is trapped, giving hope to the weary soul within.

Lift up your heads mortal man, see the light that comforts you! Even as you mourn, even in your deepest sorrows.

LORD GOD ALMIGHTY, LIGHT OF THE WORLD proclaims: Rejoice in the light, for your redemption draws near and the light contains all that you will ever need.

The light of our LOVING LORD shall suffice.

Light illuminates the soul within

Cascades down upon the weary masses

Upon the weary dust forlorn

Light shines its hope, its joy, its form

Light grows food for the hungry

Creates rain for the parched lands never seen

Shines upon the shame of the wicked

Light cannot be purchased, bribed, or stolen

It only knows freedom unbounded by man

Light returns afresh in the morning

Shaking off the weariness of those who tarry

Upon this great Earth formed in the light of creation

By the great and wonderful I Am

May the light of the world be upon you

May the joy of that light shine from above

May it carry all of your troubles to Heaven

Where His holy light will melt them with love

Sing of the light of creation!

Scroll Three

"The Song Of Wisdom"

GOD ALMIGHTY – CREATOR OF THE UNIVERSE – KING OF THE ANGEL ARMIES – LORD OF LORDS – IMMANUEL

Sings All Into Creation With Wisdom

Wisdom is the subtle answer that clarifies all things. Wisdom is found by searching out the matter through a field of chaos and a myriad of lesser choices.

Wisdom is not fleeting, for once established, wisdom becomes the beacon upon the hill that lights the path for all to navigate through treacherous waters and to reach safe harbors.

Wisdom gives guidance to the hands for obtaining the finest materials so as to create masterpieces of art, tools, methods of science and genius of application.

Wisdom gives peace where no peace can be found.

Wisdom never lies, for wisdom is the very embodiment of truth distilled down to its most basic form. Wisdom abhors corruption, for it knows that corruption destroys nations, families, and souls.

Wisdom must be requested from GOD ALMIGHTY, who is WISDOM; HE will grant it in abundance to those who will only ask specifically to be given its tremendous value and strength.

Wisdom creates wealth and vanquishes poverty, both poverty of decrepit living, but even more importantly, poverty of the spirit.

Wisdom brings and draws people to those whom shine from within by the light. Wisdom is bestowed in the very core of their being and their words that flow are an inspiration to all around.

Wisdom screams from the towers: Run for shelter! Hide from the approaching storm! Man the barricades and prepare to repulse the onslaught and tumult that approaches!

Wisdom gleans the tiniest shreds of information, divergent shards of facts, innuendo and half-truths to obtain a clear picture of the future and then prepares accordingly for that eventual outcome.

Wisdom has a soft touch, a gentle answer, a knowing sigh – and by doing so, deflects much anger and destroys with a whisper many evil intents.

Brilliant plans are laid to waste for all to see by a single grain of wisdom properly applied.

Wisdom praises GOD in all circumstances, even when the walls fall, mountains crumble, seas roar, and death is on the march, for wisdom understands that the LORD controls all things and only HE can answer with wisdom when man can find no means of escape and all is to no avail.

Wisdom holds on relentlessly to love, kindness, forgiveness, and joy and throws away that which is corrupt, foul, base and of any type of darkness that places into peril the immortal soul of mortal man.

Wisdom obtained from the LOVING GOD shall make a man's spirit soar to realms unknown and grant access to the very throne room of a benevolent and righteous SAVIOR, the KING OF KINGS and LORD OF LORDS, whom, if asked, shall forgive your sins, hear your pleas, and grant favor as only HE can.

Wisdom allows for a pleasurable rewarding life and a wonder of years to all men of all ages.

Seek wisdom and your life will be sweet as both GOD and man shall shower you with praise and surround you with Love.

Sing of wisdom!

Oh call to me wisdom

And pleasure me with love

Grant me all of your knowledge

That only comes from HIM above

Show me all your kindness

As wisdom only knows

Sow the seeds of joy

That in my gardens grow

Place me in a future

Of tremendous wealth to spare

Please allow me the wisdom

Of how, and when, and where

May all of the LORD ALMIGHTY's
Wisdom gently rain
Every day and every hour
So tremendous joys I gain

May HIS *Wisdom grant me timing*
Which in my simple hands
Knows when to vanquish evil
And when to stop and stand

Wisdom calls out to the tiny
Those who are small within our sights
Allows them to pray to GOD ALMIGHTY
To sling stones of valiant might

Wisdom calls through the ages
To all who care to hear
Lay down your toils and troubles
Give HIM *all your Earthly fears*

Scroll Four

"The Song Of Hope"

GOD ALMIGHTY – CREATOR OF THE UNIVERSE – KING OF THE ANGEL ARMIES – LORD OF LORDS – IMMANUEL

Sings All Into Creation With Hope

*Hope is a powerful force that rarely has a basis in fact or
circumstance.*

*Hope lifts the countenance of even the most distraught fallen soul,
souls of men crushed under the burdens of daily life, shattered
dreams, broken promises.*

*Hope allows a new dawn to force the most tattered amongst us to
once again start a new day with the longing belief that all will be
Well...*

Better...

Kinder...

More inspired...

Of finer quality.

Hope breaks the bonds of lingering doubts, failed missions, and dark memories.

Where there is hope, a way shall present itself to escape the current confines of delusions, dreads, and fears.

Hope rests its heel on fear and will not allow its poison to infect the future or steal the journey of life from even the weariest of souls.

Hope confines the darkness then casts it aside with ease.

One tiny grain of hope, the smallest possible portion, shall break chains of disillusion that would ensnare your tomorrows.

Hope is a journey out of your current destruction, torn relationships, and fractured dreams.

Hope rescues those who cannot be rescued...
Finds those who cannot be found...
Desires the best for those who are not desirable by any other means...

Without hope, all is beyond lost, for it is quickly forgotten and shall never be dreamed of again.

Yet, with hope, dreams become reality, love transcends all, Courage flourishes and light invades your world.
With hope kindness reigns.

With hope love abounds.

With hope, joy is your essence and success is your destiny.

Hope is a divine spark lingering within our souls, a remnant of the original divine light that burst into being by the great and mighty
I AM!

Hope is a divine remnant from GOD ALMIGHTY given as a gift that destroys the pursuit of yesterday's foibles and tomorrow's destruction.

Reach down, lift the countenance of those fallen amongst you with the brilliance of hope and this very day shall be divine.

Hope is eternal.

Hope sings the morning into love.

Hope is your portion, daily, from our FATHER who loves you beyond words, beyond measure.

Hope is a gift – do not fail to receive it.

Hope is a seed that will grow in tragic soils.

Lonely deserts...

Lost horizons...

Frozen dreams...

Thundering waters...

Hope's seed, although tiny, has the deepest roots and reaches to the very threshold of heaven's gate to bring the KING OF HEAVEN and HIS blessings in overflowing abundance to you and those you love.

Sing of hope!

I Choose Joy!

Introduction by Mathias, the '13th Apostle', of Joy Dawn to the World at Far Point

Though I arise in the morning before the dawn awakens the sky, even then at that early morning hour, I shall choose joy!

Should thunderstorms disrupt the evening's twilight with sounds of GOD ALMIGHTY announcing HIS command of the Earthly Realm, Even in the midst of those resounding proclamations, I shall choose joy!

As lightning destroys the timbers of mighty oaks standing in faraway dense forests of trees, splitting the sky with HIS fierce shrieks of dominance of the night, yes, even then, I shall choose joy!

Tornadoes of swirling maelstrom, hurricanes of relentless winds, both may overtake my mortal body and tear my world to splinters, and even in the midst of those fierce tempests, even then, I still will choose joy!

Volcanoes can cascade down mountains mighty with rivers of molten rock and fountains of doom. Displaying the very depths of Hell, even then, in the presence of their radiant heat, I shall choose Joy!

As mountains fall, I shall choose joy!

As seawalls crumble, I shall choose joy!

Rip the Earth asunder!

Release The Kracken!

Scour the shoreline barren with The Scourge that knows not the boundaries of the sea...

Bind my arms with cord...

Cut my hair...

Abandon me in the pit of broken dreams...

Fire up the furnace...

Throw my mortal body within its molten grasp...

Bear false witness against my righteous cause...

Scourge me within an inch of death...

Pound nails through my bones...

Deny me as one of your own...

But, even then, I shall choose joy!

Give me joy in the morning as the sunshine steals the dew away.

Give me joy in the noontime as the heat of the day bakes the weary Earth beneath my feet.

Give me joy when the sun sets, beyond far, over a horizon that I may never know, that I may never reach...

Joy destroys all hindrances placed upon me by lesser men that wish to steal my essence...

Steal my tomorrows...

No matter the costs, I shall choose joy!

For like love and courage, light, and wisdom, when the Earth crumbles, the sky falls, and the seas roar, only joy can be counted as the call to a higher realm.

As I live and walk upon this frail world given to me for such a short while, I will not spoil that walk with a lesser choice...

And, with total and complete disregard for the inferior path...

With every breath...

Every step...

Every desire...

Every thought...

By my very prayers to HEAVEN's KING...

I shall choose joy!

Chapter Eighteen

Joshua, now many decades older and stooped over by the relentless effects of time and gravity, slowly padded along the chiseled onyx stones of his extensive garden that was manicured and groomed to perfection. As he stepped from stone to stone, navigating as best he could, it dawned on him that his battle no longer was with time, but with gravity!

It appeared that gravity was a relentless force, which pursued him at every waking moment...

He left that unwanted wayward thought go as he opened the immaculately carved wooden double doors, created from massive slabs of priceless curly koa. They opened into the mansion he'd built, decades earlier, for the love of his life.

Joyous noises, that he had grown to love, no longer erupted from inside as they once did.

Children grow up and then leave to create lives of their own. Once he and his lovely wife, Summer, had been active participants in their children's lives. Now they had become mere observers.

That seemed like eons ago...

Joshua slowly walked among the priceless artifacts, past the photos of family and friends, all intermingled with masterpieces captured in both oil and bronze. Joshua, in his socks now, walked carefully on the polished blue gum eucalyptus hardwood floors to make his way into his den that overlooked the groomed gardens and entryway to the estate. His den overlooked the vast Atlantic Ocean, which roared and cast its waves against the sandy shoreline without remorse or care.

Their home was profoundly elegant, an architectural masterpiece. It was built with extraordinary craftsmanship from the finest materials of stone, glass, exotic woods, and ceramics fired by masters in Italy and Japan.

Allowing gravity to win, he fell into his leather chair, worn perfectly to fit him in his old age. He'd reached his den and with a click of a tiny remote, his fireplace erupted into dancing flames of pure natural gas burning translucent blue. Every time he did that simple task of using the remote to create an instantaneous fire, it made him smile. Who would have ever thought of such a thing?

He looked at a small chalkboard he kept; it was framed in koa and had but one number handwritten in green chalk within its borders. Currently it displayed the number *38*. He had achieved the completion of his *38th Cycle.* That number represented vast amounts of wealth. Wealth beyond description. Yet, only Joshua knew what it truly meant, and he was all right with that. The world could keep its accolades and he would keep his successes to himself. Due to structure and method, Joshua and Summer were the only ones that knew they had most likely become the wealthiest couple living upon the face of the earth. But, more importantly, they knew the truth, which they both held deep within their hearts. The simple reality that the only true wealth they had acquired had absolutely nothing to do with material possessions or their vast global empire.

After all, stuff was just stuff...

Joshua glanced absentmindedly at the wall map he kept constantly updated. It showed the global empire he'd been able to build with Summer by his side: Fields for wheat and hard grain production in central Kansas, and a sprawling mining operation in Goldfields, Nevada that produced gold, silver, and rhodium at obscene rates. Rare earth operations, obtaining minerals for today's world, in Africa, Asia and South America were more than profitable. They were a modern day necessity for telecommunications and satellite transmissions.

The operations included natural gas and oil production platforms, pipelines and refining facilities from the shale formations in Texas, Oklahoma, West Virginia, Ohio and Pennsylvania.

They also comprise offshore oil platforms in the Gulf of Mexico and far away in the South China Sea. Those operations included his bulk carrier fleet that moved liquid fuels to the international marketplaces of commerce and industry.

Then there was his personal favorite, another place that he also called home. Sitting high above Santiago, Chile, at the base of the mighty Andes Mountain Range, he grew table grapes in the vineyard that wrapped all the way around the villa he'd built for Summer.

He told her that it was so they could enjoy summer year round!

They raised their daughters there. GOD had been generous in gifting them with two children, the first they named April and the second they named Grace after her Grandmother Rains.

It was more than appropriate.

They were wonderful in their own unique ways; so differently marvelous, they were all that Summer and Joshua could have wished for.

They were both coming home today. They'd sent the family Learjet to pick them up from their homes in Singapore and Hong Kong. They were coming home with their husbands and their newest addition – their oldest, April, was a new mother. It was strange to even think of her as married, let alone a mother...

How oddly fast time flew by. His greatest asset was time, and at this stage of life, he could feel it slowly fading from his grasp.

Summer came into the room and stood by the fireplace smiling; she too was more than excited to have the children coming home to join them on The Bluffs.

With Summer silhouetted against the dancing blue flames, he had a vision of times long gone. Times he could barely separate now between when he was living or during that strangely intensive learning experience: *beyond the veil*. As he thought of it now, from this distant perspective of decades gone by since his incident with the crash.

Forcing himself out of the chair and overcoming his greatest foe, gravity, Joshua stood by his loving wife at the fireplace. He put his arm around her. Out of the blue, for no apparent reason other than the longings of his heart, he read the ancient text hanging on the wall. It was the *Scroll Of Love*. He read it with great enthusiasm and with an inspired heartfelt joy of the moment:

Scroll Five

"The Song Of Love"

GOD ALMIGHTY – CREATOR OF THE UNIVERSE – KING OF THE ANGEL ARMIES – LORD OF LORDS – IMMANUEL

Sings All Into Creation With Love

Love is the deepest and most abiding force in all of creation. It transcends all of creation in every realm. Love simply is. When the very first utterance and command of GOD, CREATOR OF THE UNIVERSE was spoken, it was spoken in love. Wrapped in love. Delivered in love. All that has been, is, and forever will be was breathed into its very being by that first divine act of love. HIS word set the entire essence of all things into the very bedrock of love.

Love transcends all knowledge, devours all wrongs, builds all that shall be determined to be righteous, absorbs all blows, administers all gifts and divulges – for all to witness – all that is good, pure, and beautiful.

Love is obvious and perfectly kind. Love knows no boundaries. Love pursues all peoples - until even those whom deny its very existence – until even they must admit its relentless force, a force that shall shatter the very gates of hell and free the captives from within; captives of the deepest darkness shall be saved by the light of love.

Love abhors indifference and shatters the very souls of those who practice enslavement of the Spirit that GOD has given mortal man.

Love shines best when nourished – yet even when deserted – it breaks away to soar above all wrongs and delivers itself to those most in need of its intimate companionship.

Love is the divine breath of THE ONE AND TRUE GOD, the LIVING GOD, YAHWEH, CREATOR OF THE UNIVERSE and is what makes our spirits leap, and race into an uncertain future as Children Of Light and as HIS divines sparks of love.

Should I speak softly and carry the voice of the angels with the essence of love within – all things shall be given unto me. The very power of creation shall come forth from my lips and nothing shall be able to withstand my decrees.

Darkness shall flee and the light of love shall overcome every obstacle.

To speak with the force of Love is to walk in the divine realm of heaven with the approval of the CREATOR forever across the universe of time.

Love is the original word spoken and shall sing triumphant throughout all of the ages of man.

Love is what binds us

Love is the sound that was spoken at creation

Love is kindness

Love is all that is worthy

Love is what is good, what is clean, what is pure
Love knows only righteousness and truth
Love endures beyond all tribulations
Love shall never end

Love is beyond, above, and past time itself
Love cannot be crushed or ignored
Love transcends the human mind
Love is fundamental in its existence
Love is existence in its purest form
Love is, that it is, that it is

Love is the light that shines in any darkness
Love destroys the darkness
Love hates that which is evil
Love will not be denied

Love creates the improbable and builds the impossible
Love is the joy in the morning and the hope at night
Love is frailty and crushes that which the world calls strong
Love binds wounds and heals the broken hearted
Love dries the tears of yesterday and tomorrow
Love is life and life will always find a way

Love is GOD *and* GOD *is Love*

When all things have passed away

Love will be all that remains

Love is the song of GOD, *and that song shall sing forever into the*

eons of time and through the very souls of man

Sing of love!

Chapter Nineteen

Summer reached up, grabbed Joshua gently by both cheeks, and kissed him from the depths of her heart with the passionate joy of love unbounded.

Together they had built a life together, fought sorrows, shared joys, danced and laughed, and cried and pondered.

Together they forced themselves to embrace each day with wild abandon and fearless hearts of trust in the loving GOD they served.

And today, at this very hour, they stood hand in hand as flames danced before them. Flames burning brilliant like the fire they found themselves within, the fires of time that had captured them so long ago when they had decided to share their lives, as one together, into an uncertain future.

Shortly their greatest joys would be home! Their wonderful effervescent daughters, the fine young April and her husband, and, of course the star of the show, the newest member of the family, baby Hope.

Along with their youngest, the fine young Grace and her new husband whom they hardly knew.

Summer couldn't wait to hold the newest member of the family, her first grandchild who was obviously in need of excessive spoiling. Eventually she would teach her to cook with discernment and love in the kitchen that knew nothing but the finest of ingredients, and if need be, a secret or two...

Joshua had a different plan, he was waiting to get his recently acquired sons-in-law into his den, where he could start the process of imparting lessons from *The Wisdom of*

Wealth to the next generation. It was his divine duty. It was the least he could do. He would find the time, as a gift paid towards a debt he could never repay.

A gift to his mentor, Mr. Rains, whom it appeared he had actually never met.

Turning from the fire, he strolled with his lovely wife to the front door portico. Lingering where they waited together for their greatest joys, their family, to arrive along with the hopes of a joyful dawn, all as a glorious sunrise appeared with huge beams of divine light bursting forth, from beyond the horizon of gentle clouds heralding a new day. Their children were coming home!

Arriving on silver wings with their own dreams of wondrous tomorrows...

Cherished memories...

As long as time would allow...

Chapter Twenty

Many years later, Joshua found himself searching once again to obtain the answers to a mystery that had haunted him most of his life. Where on earth - *or more appropriately heaven* - had Mr. and Mrs. Rains come from? Were they real? Had they been sent as a vision? As a dream? As a longing of his heart? As a means to steer him towards some type of special divine destiny?

This lingering quest for answers, once again, had led him back to his alma mater, to the hallowed halls of a place he knew so well. Back to Harvard's library and its vast storehouse of man's splintered knowledge captured in bits and pieces, hidden amongst endless facts, tucked away in wooden stacks of time. The shelves stood silently row upon endless row.

He slowly walked past shelves, leaning on his koa cane that glimmered occasionally as the intermittent lights illuminated it on his long journey back to the furthest reaches where the Guttenberg Bible remained alone. Yet, it spoke with a divine purpose that proclaimed for all that would choose to see: true courage, true light, true wisdom, true hope, and true joy that a loving GOD had entrusted to a world that surely needed it's lesson of true love more than it cared to learn.

Joshua, always brave enough to have the courage to discover something new, went to its crystal glass case. He gazed at that ancient text printed with the purest ink. There he pulled out his latest generation iPhone and snapped a picture of the sacred book at a 'random' page opened for all to see.

He used the app - *Latin to English* - he'd downloaded for this exact mission, to see what he could discover. Within the twinkling of an eye he had his answer. All these years, the answer that he so longingly sought, had been right here. It was waiting for him to simply perform this singular task of his decades long quest for the truth. The translation so elegantly placed before him proclaimed:

1 *Let not your heart be troubled: ye believe in GOD, believe also in ME.*

2 *In MY FATHER's house are many mansions: if it were not so, I would have told you. I go to prepare a place for you.*

3 *And if I go and prepare a place for you, I will come again, and receive you unto MYSELF; that where I am, there ye may be also.* [John 14: 1-3 KJV]

Joshua smiled as he allowed the TRUTH, once again, to set him free.

Epilogue

"YOU DID WHAT!" demanded Zachariah's father at the dinner table. Ignoring the steaming hot kumu, his wife, Mai, had prepared for the evening's meal. Zachariah's mother had cooked the speared delicacy with the finest ingredients exactly as everybody loved it. She stuffed it with shredded bamboo shoots along with sliced shiitake mushrooms, baked it to perfection, then caramelized it by pouring boiling peanut oil, shoyu, fresh ginger and brown sugar over the prized catch just prior to serving.

A master chef could have done no better.

All of that mattered not. Nalu Rains, the acting Governor of the Great State of Hawaii was demanding an answer of why his son, who knew better, would ever go diving by himself? And, of all places, at *Heaven's Threshold!* The name said it all – many souls had been lost there. It was like *Far Point* on Kauai, both areas were unforgiving ocean wilderness; they were amongst the most treacherous dive sites on GOD's blue planet.

"By yourself? For a fish?" Zachariah's father was exasperated, demanding some type of answer.

"Well, I did bump into a tourist while I was out there..."

Zachariah and his parents ate most of the meal in complete silence. The kumu was delicious, but there really wasn't much to say. They both loved their youngest son immensely and hated to see him take such profoundly dangerous risks. Especially scuba diving alone in the vast Pacific, which was totally unacceptable.

Zachariah, of course, failed to tell them what really happened, namely that he became trapped, ran out of air, and almost died was not going to help his position in any way.

After the meal, Zachariah went back to his room. He told his mum and dad that he needed to study for a while. But, what he really needed, was air and some time...

After all, he was still trying to come to terms with seeing a mighty being of light beside a young man on a shelf of lava rock overlooking the bay. The angel shown like the sun! The young man, who was sitting beside him, wore a faded blue hospital gown! Yet, he was the exact same young man that had saved his life – not once – but twice!

Neither of them seemed to have a care in the world. It was otherworldly and very strange.

Zachariah sat on the edge of his bed completely mystified, as he twirled the SpareAir bottle in his hands – *that he did not own* – a truth that transcended all of the facts that he would ever know...

The Epic Journey

A New Novel:

The Gold Illu$ion

"Summer Rains"

&

A Newer Novel:

The Leatherwood

A Historically Inaccurate Novel Gone Wondrously Astray

Made in the USA
Middletown, DE
03 January 2023